THE TWO OF US

THE TWO OF US

CLAUDE BERRI   Drawings by Lydia Rosier

TRANSLATED FROM THE FRENCH BY HELEN WEAVER
William Morrow and Company, Inc.   New York 1968

Published simultaneously in Canada by George J. McLeod Limited, Toronto.

Printed in the United States of America.

Library of Congress Catalog Card Number 68-54412

THE TWO OF US

It was November in Nemours. We had left Paris because there was a war on and we were Jewish. My father was from Poland and my mother was from Rumania. They were furriers. They loved each other and I was born. I was happy. I did whatever I liked and I was always getting in trouble. It was wonderful. When he talked about me, my father would throw up his hands as if to say there was nothing he could do and my mother would smile at his confusion as if she had played a good trick on him by bringing me into the world. I was happy. So were my parents. In spite of all the trouble I caused them, and even though we were poor. But they loved each other and they loved me. And there were always friends in the house.

One day my father spoke to me in a voice that I had never heard before, a voice that came from very far away. His face was handsomer than usual and his eyes were tenderer. He told me that I would have to be good now. Because there was a war on, and because we were Jewish. My mother talked to me too. She told me that war was a terrible thing and that to be Jewish when there was a

[7]

war was even more terrible. That I would have to be good. Because otherwise she might die and so might Papa. I did not want my parents to die. I cried. I promised to be good. As good as gold. As good as the smartest kid in class, whom I couldn't stand. Because I was Jewish and because there was a war on.

Unfortunately, I wasn't used to being good.

• • • •

It was raining in Nemours. School was over. A German soldier was lounging in front of a shop window. Huddled in our hooded capes, Tiberius and I were planning our escapade. Our minds were made up, we would do it today. For days we had been dreaming about a tank we had seen in the toy department of the dime store on Rue Voltaire. Tiberius kept watch. I did the rest. The next thing we knew, we were at the police station.

The tank sat in state on the desk of the chief of police. We were terrified. We couldn't tell whether the police chief's smile was mean or nice. We were hiding under our capes. Tiberius was crying. I was beyond tears. The clock struck six and it was like being hit in the stomach. The police chief lit a match and it was an explosion. I thought about my parents.

Tiberius's father arrived first and pounced on his son. Now I was alone. The police chief toyed with the tank. He looked at the time. I decided he was in a hurry and I told myself that there was hope. My father came in. I threw him a desperate look. He showed his papers and I heard the police chief say that I was a troublemaker.

It was raining in Nemours. I took my father's hand. He squeezed my hand very hard and I noticed that he was trembling. A German patrol marched by. Their steps were loud in the stillness of the night.

· · · ·

We lived in a room which we used as bedroom, kitchen, and furrier's shop. A candelabra with seven candlesticks cast a faint light on the whitewashed walls. My father was spanking me. My mother was crying. The dressmaker's dummy seemed to understand. I was very unhappy. I was sorry for what I had done. I promised myself that I would be good and I accepted my punishment without a word. When it was over I pulled up my pants.

"A public nuisance."

My father threw up his hands in that gesture of helplessness which usually made my mother smile.

"A real public nuisance . . . How long is this going to go on? . . . How long? . . . For a tank. For a tank we could all have gotten caught."

He sank into a chair and put his face in his hands. He looked so unhappy that I wanted to console him.

"Calm yourself. Eat," my mother told him.

"I'm not hungry. Your son has given me a bellyful."

I was hungry. Ravenously I drank the soup which my mother fed with a spoon. It was salty from the tears I couldn't hold back.

There was a silence, which made me feel better. Then my father moaned like a wounded animal.

"How long are you going to go on feeding him with a spoon?"

To prove my good will, I took the spoon out of my mother's hands. My father tried not to smile. He sat down next to me and talked to me in a gentle voice.

[9]

"Do you want to get us all arrested? Is that what you want? Is our life too safe for you? It's not enough to be afraid of the postman or the milkman? Afraid of being turned in for a yes or a no? You think we have to attract more attention by stealing tanks? You think it's not enough as it is? You think we don't have enough troubles?"

I ate my soup all by myself and I listened as seriously as I could.

"Why did you do it? . . . Do you want us to die?"

I put my arms around his neck. The idea that he could die and that it might be my fault terrified me. He took me in his arms. My mother cleared the table. She left my father's plate. Sooner or later, he always ate.

"You think we don't make enough sacrifices for you? Didn't I give you a fire engine, Indians, private lessons in math and spelling? We don't make enough sacrifices for you? You have to have a tank yet?"

I had cried myself out. I couldn't keep my eyes open. My mother handed me my pajamas. She didn't have to rock me that night.

"What's so good about a tank, anyway?"

He always had the last word. And on this word I fell asleep.

A nightmare woke me up. I was afraid, but I didn't wake my parents. A ray of moonlight came through the window and made a little light in the room. My father and mother were sleeping with their arms around each other, as if to give each other courage. They were very beautiful. I said to myself that I loved them, and it was the first time I was aware of it. Usually I never thought

[10]

about it, or else it was because I thought about it all the time. I don't know. This thought consoled me and I wasn't afraid anymore. I went over and kissed them very softly. So they wouldn't wake up. Then I went back to bed.

. . . .

The next day we were leaving town. I had stolen a tank and the chief of police knew our identity. My father didn't scold me anymore and in the train I behaved myself. I adored trains and traveling. I could sit for hours with my nose pressed to the windowpane, watching the countryside go by. It was a beautiful day. I wasn't sorry we were leaving Nemours. And I promised myself I wouldn't steal any more tanks in big stores.

My parents smiled at me as if my quietness reassured them. The train stopped at a station and my father bought me some candy. When I was tired of looking at the countryside I looked at the people. They looked sad, and I told myself that it was because of the war.

It was getting dark when we arrived at Caluires. The house my parents had rented looked out on a gray courtyard. There were children my age. That cheered me up. Right away I made friends with René, a kid twelve years old. My father looked worried. But my mother took him away to help her fix up the house. My mother would never have dreamed of going to bed in a house that wasn't clean.

"Where she's been, you can eat off the floor," my father always used to say.

My mother was a busy little bee, she never got tired. By the time she handed me my pajamas, everything in

[11]

the house was in order. Before she went to bed and while my father was already asleep, she worked on a mink coat. War or no war, Jewish or not Jewish, we had to eat.

I liked Caluires and René became my friend. He was three years older than me and he taught me things. I was a real devil but I was very innocent. And when René told me how babies are born, I refused to believe that my parents could have done anything like that. This amused him and I began to cry. My father and mother comforted me but they never knew why I was crying. Since René knew a lot of things, I asked him what he thought of the Jews. He didn't know anything about it. I was disappointed. My father's explanations didn't satisfy me. According to him, being Jewish meant you had to be good because there was a war on. I wondered if this wasn't some kind of a trick to make me behave. Anyway, I promised myself to ask him for further explanations.

The first time René showed me how to smoke, I threw up. Then I got used to it.

My parents were happy, I was good. I had been good for a month, my parents couldn't get over it. Neither could I.

• • • •

They didn't taste very good, but René and I smoked cigarettes made of chestnut leaves in the outhouse in the courtyard.

The door had a hole in it the shape of a heart. The smoke went out the hole. The landlady banged on the door. I coughed. René put his hand over my mouth.

"Is anyone there?"

[12]

I was choking. The banging got louder. René didn't let go of me. The smoke was leaking out through the heart carved in the door.

"I don't believe it. Is someone there? Answer if there's someone there! Is it you, Mr. Langmann? You've been in there half an hour!"

When there was no answer she ventured to peek through the heart.

"It's you, René. Open the door!"

We threw our cigarettes down the hole. The door opened, revealing the indignant face of the landlady, who swore that she'd tell our parents.

I'd been good for a month.

• • • •

My mother tried to get between us. My father was on one side of the table and I was on the other. I was cornered and he was beside himself.

"But what were you doing in the toilet? What were you doing?"

"A disaster, a real disaster, a son like you." He tried to hit me, but my mother got between us.

"Leave me alone. Leave me alone. I want to know what goes on inside of him."

"Look at yourself and you'll see what goes on inside of him."

My father was speechless. I took heart again. Disarmed, he gave up.

"She's still defending him!"

He paced up and down the attic, talking to himself. "With a landlady like ours!"

On that point I agreed with him. I didn't like that old bag.

My mother came over to me. "What were you doing in the toilet?"

"Playing."

"What were you playing?"

My father threw up his hands. "She asks him what he was playing!"

I looked down. "Nothing."

My father dropped his hands. "Nothing. He has to play nothing in the toilet yet . . . And we'll all be in the street or in the ground because he has to play nothing."

"Be quiet," my mother told him.

"That's right, take his side . . . Go and play nothing with him in the toilet."

My mother decided that she could not go on defending me. She asked me gently, "Tell Mama what you were doing."

I hesitated, then replied, "Smoking."

My father sank into a chair. "So now he smokes."

That was all he said. He seemed to have given up. I sat on his lap and promised him I would be good. He smiled sadly. He ran his hand through my hair as if he had no choice but to love me in spite of everything.

· · · ·

My schoolmates liked to play war. For them war was a game. For me it was very serious. I still didn't really understand why. But I knew I had to be good while the war was on because I was Jewish. Otherwise something bad would happen to my parents.

· · · ·

The flag with the swastika waved over the fort. They were changing the guard.

In the bushes nearby, we were lying in wait for the enemy. We had picked this place to play because it was more fun. The enemy appeared and the battle began under the amused eyes of the sentries.

My enemy was nearsighted, and he lost his glasses in the scuffle. I hit him a backhand blow with my wooden sword.

"Dirty Jew!"

The insult was like an explosion. I stood paralyzed and did not press my advantage.

"Dirty Jew": those words blared in my ears. I didn't understand. For me he was the kid I played war with one day and marbles the next. I liked this fat little boy with his glasses and his faraway look. "Dirty Jew." I couldn't even get angry. I didn't understand.

I cried as I walked down on the sunken road that led to the house. I said to myself that my parents were right, that people didn't like our kind. And that it really must be dangerous to be one of us. Especially when there was a war on, as Papa said, and when you weren't a good boy. I pulled myself together and swallowed my tears. For the first time in my life, I felt Jewish. But in my mind, which was the mind of a nine-year-old, I still didn't understand. All I knew was that I had to be good. And for the first time a feeling of strength and truth went through me.

• • • •

I wasn't hungry that night. My father realized that something was wrong and asked me what had happened. I told him.

"Who is this pal?"

My father was ready for action. With me in the house, there was never a moment's peace.

"He's not a pal."

That was news to me. I thought he was one.

"But why do you think I ask you to come right home after school? . . . Why don't you listen to me? . . . Why do you have to hang around?"

"To play."

"Do I play?"

Having run out of arguments, my father was being unfair. He realized it and tried to appeal to my reason.

"When are you going to understand the situation? When are you going to be good? Don't you understand that the less people see of us, the better it is? Don't you understand that every minute we are in danger of being rounded up? Don't you love Mama? Don't you love Papa?"

I began to cry.

"What do you need to play outside? Isn't it better to do your homework? To be first in your class?"

I looked up and fought back my tears.

"Don't I have the right to play like other children?"

I was filled with a burning anger. I didn't understand. Children are supposed to play. All children play.

"After the war you can do whatever you like . . . you can play outdoors."

I told myself that after the war I might be too grown-up to play. And what if this war lasted a hundred years, like the one I had heard about in school? My mother tried to make me eat. I refused. I was sick of turnips. Besides, I was sad.

[17]

"I'll make him eat." My father sat down beside me. I gave him my terms.

"Then tell me about Mickey the Tailor, Papa."

I adored Mickey the Tailor. No sadness could hold out against a story about Mickey the Tailor. For a story about Mickey the Tailor I was capable of doing my homework ahead of time, taking down the garbage, running races, even eating turnips. Mickey the Tailor made me good again. I loved him. He was part of my life. If he had walked into the house one day, I wouldn't have been surprised. This had been going on for years. My father had exhausted all the resources of the character. He had served Mickey the Tailor with every possible sauce. With him he had told me about his childhood in Poland, the sleighs, the white plains, growing up in Paris, his friends, his struggles, how he met my mother, and how they fell in love. Because of Mickey the Tailor I knew all about loyalty, love, and tenderness. Through him I had learned about the seriousness of friendship, the necessity for courage, the joy of accomplishment, and the uncertainty of power. He had taught me to notice the smells of the country, the ray of sunlight on the table while my mother ironed—busy little bee that she was. What others have learned from books or from life itself, Mickey the Tailor taught me through the magic of a father's love for his child.

"Mickey the Tailor had a son like you . . . who wouldn't eat his turnips without being coaxed . . . who wouldn't mind his papa and his mama . . . a son who gave him a lot of aggravation . . . Mickey the Tailor didn't know what to do with his son . . . to make his son behave, to make him understand the situation."

[18]

"Was Mickey the Tailor Jewish?"

"Of course."

"And his son too?"

"Of course."

I ate my turnips and listened gravely. My father looked happy. I imagine he must have been counting on Mickey the Tailor to make me understand "the situation," as he called it, once and for all.

"There was a war on and Mickey the Tailor's son refused to understand the situation . . . refused to understand that he must come right home after school . . . that he couldn't play outside . . . that he must be good . . . learn to eat by himself . . . to wash by himself . . . to make his own bed . . . to help his mother a little . . . Mickey the Tailor didn't know what to do to make his son understand. When he was nice to his son, his son was bad. When he was mean to his son, his son was bad too. . . ."

Mickey the Tailor and the little fat boy had helped me to understand. That night when I went to bed I promised myself that I would really be good. The war wouldn't last forever. And I would have to be patient. Later I would play. I was sad, but my mind was made up. Besides, I was sure that Mickey the Tailor would help me be good. My parents kissed me. Then they went to visit their friend Raymonde who lived down the hall. I went to sleep.

• • • •

The sirens woke me up. Their wail terrified me. I lay paralyzed in my bed, unable to move a muscle or utter a sound. If somebody had cut my heart out with a knife, I wouldn't have bled.

[19]

My mother ran into the room and picked me up. Silently I pressed myself against the warmth of her body, and this made me feel better.

A ray of moonlight streamed through the air shaft and lit the cellar. In the distance, bombs were falling. Some of the women were praying. Others were weeping. Some were very brave. The men were talking about the war. Some said it would soon be over. Others said it would be long. I agreed with the first. I convinced myself that they were right. That way I could play in peace. I wasn't afraid. My father and mother were there. When I was with them I felt that nothing could happen to me. They were calm. Their friend Raymonde was with them. Her face had lines in it but it was beautiful. I liked her because my parents did. A cat jumped into my lap and I petted it. The scream of the sirens announced the all clear and my blood froze again.

I buried my face in my mother's neck until the noise had stopped. Outside the night was clear and we all went back to our homes.

· · · ·

Because my parents were worried about me, Raymonde had offered to take me to the country to stay with her father, who was a fine old man. My parents had accepted.

· · · ·

The thought of leaving my parents was unbearable. I didn't go out to play the last few days before my departure. I didn't feel like it. I stayed with my parents. I wanted to make the most of the little time I had left. But I understood. I hadn't complained. I was a man now. I gritted my teeth. I didn't let them see me cry.

I did it secretly. I went inside the toilet, but not to smoke cigarettes made of chestnut leaves. I cried silently so as not to attract attention. Then I went and washed my face at the tap in the courtyard. My parents told me that the country was beautiful down there. They said that I would be happy, and that they would come and get me when the war was over. And that afterwards we would be happy all the time. They congratulated me on my courage, and told me that Mickey the Tailor would have been proud of me.

The train was there and my heart was heavy. It was raining in Caluires and it was cold. It was January. The German soldiers made green spots in the crowd. The people were sad. I told myself that when I grew up I would never go to war, and that if everybody else did the same, there wouldn't be any little boys on station platforms saying goodbye to their parents.

In the compartment Raymonde was looking after the baggage. I was on the platform with my parents. My mother stared straight ahead as if she were afraid to look at me, afraid she would lose her courage. My father took me in his arms.

"Do you know your name?"

"Yes, Papa: Claude Longet."

"No. Not Longet . . . Longuet . . . understand? . . . Longuet . . . Longuet . . . It's easy!"

"Yes, Papa."

"How do you spell Longuet?"

"L . . . O . . . N . . . G . . . E . . ."

"No! LONGUET. Longuet . . . like a *longuet** . . ."

"What's a *longuet?*"

* small, narrow loaf of bread—*Translator.*

[21]

My father put me down and threw up his hands, the way he always did when he didn't understand. God knows, I had given him enough opportunities not to understand. I really was a funny kid.

Some German soldiers walked right by us. My mother bent down.

"Pay attention, my darling . . . It says Longuet on your ration book . . . Longuet."

I burst into tears. They were asking too much of me. It was hard enough being brave . . . If I had to learn to spell too! I fought back my tears. My father took over. My mother stared ahead of her again to keep from breaking down.

"At your age, you have to know your name!"

"Yes, but it isn't my name."

"Until the end of the war, it is your name, do you understand?" The people were hurrying. It was almost time. A voice rang out over the loudspeaker.

"All passengers for the train to Grenoble . . . Please get on board."

My mother took me in her arms and hugged me so hard it hurt.

"After the war, will I have my own name back?"

"Yes, my darling. After the war your name will be Langmann again forever . . . forever. . . ."

Her voice sounded funny. She put me in my father's arms and stared ahead of her again. My father walked toward the door to the car.

"Do you remember the prayer Raymonde taught you?"

"Yes, Papa."

I mustered all the courage I had left and murmured, "Our Father which art in heaven, hallowed by thy name

. . . thy kingdom come . . . thy will be done, on earth as it is in heaven. . . ."

He set me down on the steps of the train

"Give us . . ." I stopped. I couldn't go on. My father looked at me pleadingly.

"Give us what?"

I told myself that I'd have plenty of time to practice the prayer on the train. I said, "Kiss me."

He kissed me. Then Raymonde came and took me into the compartment.

I was standing at the window of the compartment, holding my head in my hands. My father and mother had their arms around each other. They only had each other now and they were paralyzed with grief. They looked very beautiful and I thought how much I loved them. I winked at them to cheer them up. This was when the tears came and the train started to move. Everything happened very fast. I saw my father dash forward. He rummaged in his pockets as he ran and handed me his pocket watch through the window. My mother was standing very straight. My father was panting in time to the train. Then he stopped and saluted me like one man to another. The train whistled. My parents disappeared. I held the pocket watch to my ear and felt as if I were hearing my father's heart beating.

• • • •

I liked Raymonde because my parents liked her. She was a great comfort to me during the trip. It was like having a little bit of my parents still with me. She made me practice the "Our Father" and taught me another prayer about a lady named Mary. I slept through the trip because I was very tired.

[23]

· · · ·

As we walked up the path that led to her father's house, Raymonde made me repeat my prayers and spell my new name. I had learned my lesson well and this reassured her. A frightened rabbit dashed against our legs. For a moment I was happy. The country smelled good.

· · · ·

He was enormous and he stooped, as much from height as from age. A proud little moustache covered up his lips. His eyes were sleepy and sly with a childish little glint deep down. His mouth was sad. He wasn't handsome, but I told myself that he was so old that he couldn't be mean. His ears were much too big. They were also hairy and stuck out. His nose was flabby. His face was jowly. But it was his arms that really fascinated me. There was no end to them. And since he stooped when he walked, they almost seemed to touch the ground. He reminded me of the gorilla I had liked so much in the zoo. Papa had even scolded me about it. He couldn't understand why I liked gorillas when there were animals like gazelles or marmosets. Maybe it was because of the gorilla in the zoo whom I liked so much that I was not afraid of the old man. It was also because my parents couldn't send me to live with anybody who was bad. But why didn't he like Jews? This was what I was thinking about when he asked me my name.

"My name is Claude, Monsieur . . . Claude Longet . . ." I spelled it: "L-O-N-G-U-E-T."

The old man looked at me with his old eyes.

"It's spelled Longuet and it's pronounced Longet?"

I thought he acted a little suspicious and I realized

[24]

my mistake. I felt a stab of fear but I decided to keep right on going.

"Yes, M'sieu."

He smiled at me and I was afraid he would try to find out more about it.

"Call me Pépé."

I was relieved. I smiled back at him.

Mémé was a little old woman with a face as wrinkled as an apple. She seemed to be the opposite of the old man. But since they had been living together forever, they had ended up looking like each other. He dominated her but she treated him like a child, although she was clever enough not to let it show. Her character was less definite than that of the old man and I realized at once that she would be nice to me.

Still, I felt that this old man and his wife were not happy. I sensed these things the way children do. They seemed sad. And I thought of my parents, who I knew were each half of the same person.

Kinou was the dog. He was at death's door. I saw at once that he was part of the family.

Still, when we went to the table, I was surprised that he had a place set for him and that he sat beside the old man, who tied a bib around his neck.

"His name is Kinou . . . He's not so young anymore, you know . . . He's fifteen . . . Fifteen last month . . . The seventeenth of December . . . We had some party, didn't we, Kinou? . . . Seven times fifteen. He's not so young anymore . . . Ah, when he was your age . . . he could go upstairs all by himself . . . At Rue de Belleville we had six flights . . . You should have seen him . . . Four at a time. . . ."

"Why seven times fifteen?"

The old man waved his hand wearily, then held Kinou's soup spoon to his muzzle.

"That's how it is . . . For every year we live, they live seven. . . ."

He looked sad, and I realized that he loved his dog. And this made me like him more. He noticed the look on my face and I think he understood it.

Mémé had set a steaming, fragrant rabbit on the table. My mouth watered. It had been a long time since I had eaten rabbit. The old man was a vegetarian. He passed up the stew for a plate of vegetables. He threw me a disapproving look, which didn't make a dent on my appetite.

"I eat vegetables . . . nothing but vegetables."

I began eating ravenously and paid no attention to his vegetarian act of faith. Mémé was searching in the head with the point of her knife. The silence was total. Wishing to draw attention to himself, the old man attacked: "I respect life . . . What's the point of hanging around the priest all the time if you have no respect for life?"

Mémé and Raymonde exchanged knowing looks. Mémé played the victim with an ill grace.

"You see . . . Your father hasn't changed . . . He's always criticizing me . . . He treats me like a beast of burden. . . ."

The old man didn't miss the opportunity and muttered, as if with regret, "If only you were."

"We're lucky we have our rabbits . . . Otherwise, what would we eat?"

"Vegetables!"

Mémé shrugged her shoulders. Obviously she had long since given up trying to convince him of anything.

"Do you really like rabbit?"

Did I like it! I loved it! It was a far cry from turnips. But the look he gave me made me look down in shame. Still, I kept on devouring the fragrant meat.

"Yes, M'sieu."

"Then you're a cannibal like the rest." I didn't feel guilty, but I didn't want to disappoint him. I controlled my appetite.

Raymonde intervened. "Stop, Papa. Let the child eat in peace! For once when he has something on his plate."

Raymonde had influence with her father and he was quiet for a few minutes. I took advantage of this silence to polish off what was left on my plate. The old man broke the silence.

"Aren't there any vegetables in town?"

"Yes, turnips and salsify roots. Pig food."

"Is it my fault if there's a war on?"

"Well, it certainly isn't his, Papa . . . So let him eat in peace."

I had finished eating and I was observing the old man. He seemed quite upset. I listened carefully to what he was telling me.

"You never see the ones whose fault it is . . . They're safe and sound, in London or someplace . . . They don't know anything about rationing . . . It's always the little guys who get the worst of it . . . They don't get bombs in their faces, the ones whose fault it is. They're the ones who drop them . . . And what a mess! . . . When they're aiming for the station, they destroy the church

. . . When they're aiming for the church, they destroy the station."

I wondered what all this had to do with the rabbit. But I didn't open my mouth.

"The main thing is that they don't fall on you," said Raymonde.

"That's all I need!"

The old man was genuinely outraged and Raymonde smiled.

Mémé put in her two cents. "Where did you hear that they aim for the churches?"

He looked at her indulgently. "Anyway, they don't aim for the synagogues."

I pricked up my ears. This was it. Raymonde looked at me tenderly.

"Papa!"

He scowled and became sarcastic. "Oh, excuse me! I was forgetting that you like them . . . The Popular Front . . . Blum . . . That didn't teach you your lesson . . . How many Jews were there in 'thirty-nine, out of forty million Frenchmen? Do you want me to tell you? Three percent. And how many were there in the government? Do you want me to tell you? Eighty percent. And you wonder who is responsible . . . you wonder who it is?"

His indignation was real and I got scared. But Raymonde's amused smile reassured me.

"The main thing is that they're not under your roof," she told him.

The old man threw up his hands and I thought of my father. ·

"That's all I need!"

[29]

The alarm clock went off.

"It's time," he said, leaving the table. On the way he ran his hand through my hair with real affection. He sat down beside the radio and turned it on. Over the radio there was a photograph of Marshal Pétain. The old man filled his pipe while the announcer introduced a gentleman named Philippe Henriot. He had a nice voice, but he didn't like Jews.

I had a room of my own. Mémé heard my prayer, kissed me, and wished me good night. I didn't fall asleep right away. I couldn't understand what went on in people's heads. It was too complicated for me. Why didn't Pépé like Jews, although he adored his dog? And that Monsieur Henriot, who had such a nice voice, what did he have against us? And the little fat boy I fought with at school . . . what difference could it make to him that I was Jewish? Before the war the question had never occurred to me. There were the people I liked and the others. But I didn't have anything against the others. Just because I didn't like them didn't mean I had anything against them. You can't like everybody. You like the people you like, and the others are the way they are, and that's the way it is. If everybody was like Mickey the Tailor, things would be so much simpler.

I couldn't get to sleep, so I decided to write my parents.

"Dearest Mama and Papa,
Pépé is very nice and so is Mémé. There is a dog named Kinou who eats at the table with us. I ate a rabbit. It was very good. In my room there is a gentleman with no clothes on on

a cross over my bed and flowers on the walls. I am not too sad and I love you.

Claude."

I was very sad. I missed my parents. Mickey the Tailor wasn't there anymore. I was cold. The wind rattled the windowpanes. I was alone. I put my arms around my pillow as if it were a person. I struggled against the empty feeling. I looked for the faces of my parents in the flowers on the wallpaper. I tried not to cry. I didn't want anyone to know. I would have to defend myself all alone. I told myself over and over that the war would be over someday and that I would be happy. Finally sleep overcame me.

• • • •

Mémé opened the shutters and the daylight woke me up.

"Time to get up, little bunny."

At first I didn't know where I was. And then I remembered. I got up and dressed—all by myself. I was sad. I was clumsy. Usually it was Mama who washed me. Just as it was she who fed me and made my bed.

"How long are you going to go on feeding him with a spoon?" I could hear my father's voice. Its tone was a mixture of anger and love. I made my bed by myself. I hated it. "As you make your bed, so will you lie in it," my father used to say. And when I looked at the way I had made it, I knew that I would sleep badly that night. I remembered the way my mother smoothed the white sheets with the palm of her hand. The most ordinary gesture reminded me of my parents. Their absence made me love them more . . . and I said to my-

[31]

self that it would be very hard to live without them until the end of the war.

• • • •

The kitchen looked onto the garden. It was raining. I could smell the ground. Mémé put a large bowl of milk and some bread and butter on the table. I decided that the food was much better in the country than it was in the city. That was all to the good. But if I had my choice, I would rather have eaten turnips with my parents. Still, I had a good appetite and I enjoyed my breakfast. When I had finished, Mémé handed me a tray and asked me to take it up to Pépé's room, for he always had his coffee in bed.

The old man sat in state in the middle of a big country bed. A nightcap hung over one ear and he was wearing a nightshirt. There was a picture of him dressed as a Zouave hanging over the bed. Kinou was beside him. The old man greeted me with the sound of a bugle, which he imitated by cupping his hands over his mouth like a loudspeaker. He was ridiculous but I didn't feel like laughing.

"Well, Kinou. Nothing to report? The night was calm?" Kinou licked himself. I didn't understand how anybody could sleep with a dog, especially a big dog like Kinou. I put the tray down on the bed.

The old man was propped up among his pillows. He seemed pleased with himself. You could see that he was used to being waited on. I said to myself that he must be selfish and that my father would never have let my mother bring him his coffee in bed. I promised myself that I would do it for my parents on Thursday when I didn't have to go to school, and on Sunday too.

The old man examined his bowl of coffee and made a face.

"Hmm . . . It's a little black today. Tomorrow, ask Mémé to put in a little more milk . . . will you?"

I answered "Yes" without much conviction. He annoyed me with his demands. Still, he was entertaining. Kinou barked and the old man handed him a piece of bread and butter. A smell of browning onions rose from the kitchen. Mémé was at her stove.

• • • •

I couldn't miss it. The school was straight ahead. All I had to do was follow the road that ran along the house. It was still raining. It rained the same way it had in Nemours and Caluires. It was the same fine but steady rain. It was enough to make me sad all by itself. The sky was so dark you couldn't see the mountain. As I walked by the church an old woman stared at me. I began to feel anxious. Everything frightened me. My parents weren't there, and I was afraid of everything. I was alone on the long road. And I was alone in the world. Tears ran slowly down my face. I didn't wipe them away. I was also afraid of what was going to happen in school. I wondered whether the teacher would be a man or a woman, and whether he or she would be nice. I wondered whether they would taunt me for being Jewish. I wondered what country boys were like. I promised myself that I would work, that I would be first in everything to please my parents. Besides, if I worked hard, I wouldn't have time to be unhappy.

The school was on a little square with a sycamore tree and a fountain. I sat down on a little wall at a distance from the boys and girls, who were staring at me and talking in low voices. The schoolmistress arrived. I thought she looked like a black eel. Papa and I often played the game of resemblances between animals and people. I still had the habit. I didn't like eels very much: they slip through your fingers and they're slimy.

The schoolmistress walked toward me. She had a swaying walk that made me nervous. I decided that she also looked like an umbrella, a black umbrella. The schoolmistress was completely black—her eyes, her hair, her dress, everything was black. Even her smile made me nervous. I had the feeling she was going to play a cruel joke on me. She asked me my name.

"Longuet, Ma'am."

I spelled it carefully. "L-O-N-G-U-E-T."

I hadn't made a mistake. I was proud of myself. The schoolchildren had grown bolder and were standing around us. She gave a nasty little laugh.

"That's a funny name!"

Laughter exploded around me. I looked at the ground. It's true that it was a funny name. But what could I do about it? There was a war on and I was Jewish. My real name was Langmann, a big, warm, beautiful name, my father's name, the name he had given my mother the day they fell in love, the name they gave me the day I was born, my name, my name before the war. I felt like shouting it.

When I looked up, I met the eyes of a little girl. She was blond. Her blue eyes were as transparent as water. Her little lips were like cherries. Her face was very pale. She was fragile . . . fragile . . . in her big wooden shoes and her rough clothes . . . She was so fragile that

I wanted to protect her . . . She was looking at me tenderly.

The schoolmistress clapped her hands and we went into the classroom. Without thinking about it, I sat down beside the little girl.

The classroom had the same smell as the ones I had known before, a smell of ink and modeling clay. The big stove hummed. It was warm. I felt better, partly because I was next to the little girl. I asked her her name.

"Dinou."

I liked this name. I liked the sound of it. She had smiled as she told it to me. I was happy. I got out my pencil box, my notebook, everything. I felt like being quiet, like working and sitting next to Dinou. I couldn't wait to find out whether the lesson would be in history or in arithmetic, and I hoped it would be history because I loved history. The teacher who looked so much like an eel was scratching her head and I wondered why. I thought to myself that maybe she was trying to decide between history and arithmetic.

The teacher was coming toward me. Her smile made me nervous. When she was standing beside me she ran her hand roughly through my hair and brandished a pair of clippers which she had taken out of the pocket of her apron.

"Let's see if the Parisian has any cooties."

I couldn't stand the touch of her hand. I didn't move a muscle. I was like a bird in front of a snake. She smiled. That smile had been fastened to her lips forever.

"The city cooties and the country cooties. . . ."

She let go of me. I started breathing again.

"Well, I guess it will do for today . . . You don't want to be clipped, do you?"

"No, Ma'am."

It was then that I noticed that there were some pupils whose heads were completely shaved. The sight made my blood run cold. And the thought that I might meet the same fate filled me with distress. A spitball struck me in the face. I turned around. One of the shaved heads was delightedly boasting of his exploit. The teacher continued her inspection. A child challenged me: "Paris brat, scaredy cat."

Another took it up: "Paris stupe, nincompoop."

They thought this was funny. My anger drowned out my sadness. But I controlled myself.

Cruelty was taking another form. They weren't taunting me for being Jewish, but for being a Parisian. In Paris if I'd been from the country, they would have called me a hick. Where were you, Mickey the Tailor, you who taught me to appreciate the beauty of life? When will you return and tell me about the plains of Poland and the oak trees in the forest, about the moving of flocks and the rivers that water the earth? When will you return and tell me about men and love?

The teacher had triumphed. She had found a victim. The kid she was clipping was shrieking loudly while the others laughed. Seeing that I was afraid, Dinou asked me my name. In this way she let me know that the spectacle didn't interest her, but it was also her way of helping me out.

• • • •

"No, my boy, I'm not exaggerating. A hundred and

eighty-four . . . and big ones . . . Because in 'eighteen
. . . there weren't as many as in 'seventeen . . . but they
were bigger . . . You should have seen them . . . Not
counting the ones that were hiding in the seam of my
pants . . . They're the hardest to get out. . . ."

I had met the old man in a woods that overlooked
the house. The rain had stopped and the afternoon was
rather pleasant.

"Did they give you Rose-Marie?"

He rolled a cigarette with a calmness that made me
feel peaceful.

"Marie-Rose," he said, correcting me.

We had collected a whole wheelbarrow full of dead
wood, and we were sitting on an old tree trunk, resting.
We could see the village below us. Smoke was coming
out of the chimneys of the houses. The old man was
dreaming about his youth. And for him too, his youth
meant war. I wondered why he talked about it with
nostalgia, and as if he missed it. No doubt it was all
of his youth that he missed. He shook his head.

"On the Chemin des Dames . . . even the Marshal
. . . just like the rest of us . . . every morning . . . he
killed them in his skivvies"

When he talked about Pétain, his voice was full of
emotion. His eyes were far away . . . as far away as his
memories . . .

He lit his cigarette.

"Just like their precious de Gaulle . . . him too, in
'sixteen, in the Thirty-third Infantry, at Douaumont,
like everybody else . . . He had to shake out his long-
johns! Just like everybody else."

This thought cheered him up. He laughed in his

[37]

sleeve. I wondered why Marshal Pétain's cooties brought tears to his eyes and General de Gaulle's made him laugh. I decided that he must love one but not the other.

After a few moments of silence he remarked, "The good thing about lice is that they are no respecter of rank." I concluded from this that the old man had a sense of justice. But the question of why he didn't like Jews was still unanswered. Kinou barked.

"All right, Kinou. We'll go."

He had spoken in a low voice and I knew that he wanted to stay, but the old man could not refuse Kinou anything. He put his hand on my shoulder in a gesture of real affection and smiled at me. He got up. I followed. Kinou led the way. Mist had settled over the valley and the village had disappeared.

• • • •

It was nice and warm in my bed and I wasn't as sad. I felt closer to the old man and besides, there was Dinou. I was in the throes of a feeling I had never had before. It had nothing to do with the feeling I had when I was with my parents or when I thought about them. And it wasn't anything like the pleasure I took in remembering my best friend or being with him. Instead, it reminded me of the feeling I had when I went on a merry-go-round and it started to go fast. I was sad and happy at the same time and I felt as if my heart were skipping a beat. It was like the feeling I got when I stood on the balcony of my friend Tiberius, who lived on the seventh floor. Or when I knew my lesson and I wanted to be called on but at the same time I was afraid I wouldn't remember it. These are the things I thought of when I thought about Dinou. I didn't understand what was happening to me and once again I wished Mickey the Tailor were there.

• • • •

The old man and I accompanied Raymonde to the station. He told her that he knew from his son Victor that she was opening her home to Jews. This was madness. We had lost the war. We had to accept the fact. We couldn't always win the way we had in 'eighteen. All resistance was futile and only made our situation worse. We ought to follow the example of Pétain. Co-operation with Germany was the only policy to follow. The Jews, the Blums and all the rest had reigned long enough. After killing Christ, they had killed France.

Raymonde flew into a terrible rage and said that instead of shooting his mouth off, her brother would do better to join the Resistance himself, that it was a disgrace not to take a stand, that she even preferred the collaborators. As for her father, she advised him to mind his own business and forget about politics at his age.

Suddenly she lifted me in her arms, squeezed me hard, and told me, "You'll be fine here with Pépé and Mémé. They are very nice."

She set me down, snatched her basket, which contained three nice rabbits, out of her father's hands, kissed him, and strode off. I was very upset. I realized that she was ashamed of her father. I thought that it must be terrible not to respect your parents. But the old man did not understand.

"But what did I say? What did I say?"

He was as unhappy as a child caught stealing cookies.

[39]

I said nothing. I felt his humiliation. Child that I was, I understood that he was even more of a child than I, and I was not afraid of him in spite of his ideas. I felt affectionate toward him and I felt as if I were playing a good joke on a friend of whom I was very fond.

. . . .

We were walking in the fields near the farm. The night was very clear. It was the hour of Kinou's constitutional. Every night we took a little walk with Kinou before going to bed. Kinou showed signs of nervousness. He walked round a tree but couldn't make up his mind. The old man looked at him fondly. He said encouragingly, "Go on, Kinou . . . go on."

But Kinou went around in circles and whined in a way that broke the old man's heart.

He crouched at the dog's side and petted him: "What's the matter, little one? Do you feel them? Poor little animal . . . The air raids make him sick . . . Every time he feels them coming, it's all over. . . ." I realized that Kinou sensed that there was going to be an air raid and that it was affecting his digestive system. The old man heaved great sighs and I felt he was carrying it too far.

"Go on, little one, don't pay any attention to them, do what you have to do."

But Kinou didn't do "what he had to do," in spite of his obvious good will and the old man's encouragements. When he had run out of arguments he got up and his long arms hung down at his sides is if he were very tired.

"You can depend on it. They're going to bomb tonight! Three weeks ago when they bombed the railroad depot in Grenoble, he knew they were coming before anybody else . . . He was sick all night long. . . ."

I was thinking that Kinou certainly had very good ears, when I noticed the almost imperceptible drone of an airplane. It took the old man longer to notice it. We were walking back to the house. Kinou was following us with his tail between his legs. When the noise reached his ears the old man stopped in his tracks, and it was with a kind of pride that he said to me, turning toward Kinou, "What did I tell you? With him you don't need a siren."

And, as if the admiration he had for his dog had gotten the best of his worry, he walked on with a livelier step.

The fire was crackling in the fireplace. Pépé put on his slippers and asked me to bring him his pipe and tobacco. Kinou was stretched out by the fire, his head on his paws. Mémé was sewing by the lamp. I was sitting on my little bench, petting Kinou. We could hear the sound of the airplanes. The old man had explained to me that the bombing took place a few miles away and that I was not to be afraid. If it weren't for the effect it had on Kinou's digestion, there would be no reason to notice it. But I thought to myself that the bombing was a serious thing, because people were going to die in a little while, a few miles away.

Kinou let me pet him, but did not take his eyes off the old man, who looked back at him as he drew on his pipe.

"If you take upon yourself all the miseries of this war, you'll never hold out, little one . . . you won't see the end of it."

I had my own share of misery, and, to tell the truth, the fate of Kinou did not worry me unduly. It was mainly to please the old man that I was nice to him. My father and Mickey the Tailor had told me that people who loved animals too much were often very unhappy.

The dull sound of the bombs reached our ears. I stood at the window looking gravely into the distance. In the distance the sky was red and people were dying. The lights went out.

"Good God! A power failure, that's all we needed . . . What a night!"

Mémé lit the kerosene lamp.

"Where are my glasses?"

She looked for them and found them on the mantelpiece. She disappeared into the kitchen and came back with a knife and a piece of yellow soap. She cut off a little piece which she whittled down with the point of her knife. The old man took Kinou in his arms and lifted him onto the table. Mémé put her glasses on her nose. Their activities attracted my attention.

"Come and hold the lamp, bunny."

I picked up the lamp and walked over. Pépé was holding Kinou by the front paws and Mémé, raising the back paws, inserted the little piece of yellow soap in the shape of a suppository in Kinou's behind. I fought to keep from laughing while Kinou howled bloody murder. When the operation was over he took off like shot before the sorrowful eyes of the old man. I put down the lamp and Mémé put away her glasses. In the distance the battle raged.

• • • •

I was awakened in the middle of the night by loud voices. I dashed into the old man's room. Mémé was in such a state of excitement that she passed me without noticing my presence. Pépé was stroking Kinou, who was lying on his bed. He was consoling him.

"Don't cry, little one . . . these things happen to everyone . . . It often happened to me in Verdun . . . and I had pants on."

I realized that Kinou had "performed." The old man apologized to me: "Usually he has time to warn us. . . ."

With a violence I had never seen in him, he leaped out of bed and hurried to the window, which he opened wide. The planes were roaring. He shook his fist at them and yelled,, "Dirty cowards! . . . Dirty cowards! . . . It's easy to be up there."

Since the wind was cold, he closed the window again and went back to Kinou.

"Someday they'll blow up the whole world with their bombs."

He propped himself up among his pillows and his face closed. His indignation was real. I felt sorry for him. Somehow this made me feel better. He was really a child. Mémé arrived with a pail and broom and cleaned up the mess. I went back to my room and lay for a long time looking at the picture of my parents which was on the night table. I couldn't get back to sleep. Through the window of my room I saw the sky filled with flames. All this fuss being made over Kinou seemed ridiculous. I imagined the faces of the men and women who were going to die under the fire that was falling from the sky, who were already dead . . . and I said to myself that grown-ups were not reasonable.

[43]

The next day was Sunday. Mémé had prepared a big basin of warm water so that I could take a bath. She was bustling about. She checked the temperature of the water and laid my clothes and a towel on a nearby chair. I stood paralyzed by the basin, with my chest bare but still wearing the bottom half of my pajamas. The situation had caught me unawares: I was circumcised. She must not notice. My parents, who had thought of everything, had not thought of that. To gain time I invented the excuse that the water was too hot, and she added a big saucepan of cold water.

"Go on. You can get in now."

She left the kitchen and I seized the opportunity to take off my pajama pants and get into the water. She came back almost immediately. I was sitting in the basin and only the top half of my body was out of the water. Mémé was in a hurry. She had to make dinner and go to mass, and Victor, her son, was due to arrive any minute.

"Stand up, little bunny! I'll wash you myself, to save time."

"I've already washed."

"Your peepee too?"

"Yes."

"When?"

"Just now."

"So fast! It must not be very clean. Come on, I'll wash you myself."

"No."

"What, you're afraid to show it to me? I've seen them before, you know. Victor was a little boy like you . . . Come on . . . we'll be late. . . "

I cowered in my basin. I knew I wouldn't let her touch me, but I didn't know how I would do it. I was ready to pretend to be mad, to tell her I could just as well do it myself. The old man got me out of this tight spot. He had put on his Sunday suit, which was black. He had on a hat, a black hat. He seemed rather ill at ease in this getup, and a little grouchy. Mémé forced him to get dressed up on Sunday and he didn't like it. He grumbled, "Well, are we going to your mass?"

Mémé lost her head. He was already ready, and she hadn't even started. She became doubly impatient with me.

"Come on, give me the washcloth!"

I was ready for anything. If she insisted, I would throw soapy water in her eyes. For a few seconds I hated her. Why didn't she mind her own business? She wasn't going to see me naked. She felt my determination and turned to the old man.

"He's afraid to show me his peepee. . . ."

He was in a bad humor and he was not interested. With a nastiness that was characteristic of him, he reminded her of his vegetarianism.

"I don't blame him. He knows what you do to animals."

Annoyed, Mémé left the room. He snickered, "No pity for cannibals."

Then he left too. I seized the opportunity to leap out of my bath and dried myself furiously. The church bells were announcing mass.

Victor's car stopped by the garden door. Mémé became even more hysterical, to the great satisfaction of the old man. It was obvious that he didn't like Sunday. Kinou brought up the rear as usual.

• • • •

At the age of thirty-five, Victor seemed completely disillusioned. Stout, with gleaming black hair, he always looked as if he had just got out of bed or were getting ready to go there. Suzanne, his wife, was faded. Kinou welcomed them vaguely and everybody kissed with mild enthusiasm. Mémé threw everything together, and we went to mass.

• • • •

I had never been inside a church. I was very interested. In the first place, it smelled good. The odor of burning incense delighted my nostrils. The people sang pretty songs and everyone was well dressed. There were statues of beautiful women and one of these, which I learned later was the Virgin Mary, looked like Dinou. Jesus was handsome too, but he had no clothes on. The priest wore a skirt, but he had a good face. He stood between two little boys dressed like girls. The people spent their time getting up and sitting down and I copied them. Then a very pretty woman, preceded by a little boy disguised as a girl, asked everyone for money. Kinou walked up and down the center aisle. I sat next to the old man, who seemed bored. Mémé, however, was in seventh heaven. She was playing with a kind of necklace whose beads looked like goat droppings. Victor was asleep. Suzanne pinched him from time to time. I was starting to get bored when I felt somebody looking at me. It was Dinou. Her eyes made me blush and I felt as if I were going down in an ele-

[47]

vator. Now I knew she looked like the Virgin Mary and this made me like the Virgin Mary. And they were both wearing the same sky blue dress. The priest got up on a kind of little balcony and everybody sat down. I was wondering what he was doing up there, when he began to talk.

"We are living in an age of lies and false prophets, a cruel age with very little love in the air and a great deal of hatred and contempt. There is pillaging, slaughter, dividing of man from man, as if God were not great enough to sort the wheat from the tares. Leave that to him. His scales are not the same as ours, and when he sends us his son, he makes him the shepherd of all the sheep, including those who wear a star in the middle of their foreheads. Do not let yourselves be taken in by words which will last for but a day. The choice of Christians is very easy. They must be on the side of the oppressed."

I didn't understand everything the priest was saying but I agreed with him. I turned around to look at Dinou. She seemed to agree with him too. I waited for her eyes to meet mine before turning back to listen to the priest again.

"For example, if Christ chose to be Jewish rather than Roman at a time when the Roman legions were occupying Judea, he must have had good reasons, on which I invite you to meditate."

The priest made a gesture with his hand as if he were saying goodbye to us and came down from his little balcony. Everybody got up and began to sing. I looked at the old man. His humor did not seem to be improving. I decided it was because the priest had defended the

[48]

Jews. I was amazed to find out that Jesus was a Jew and I think the old man was too. When they had finished singing, the people bowed their heads and some even got on their knees. The smell of the incense got stronger and I took a good whiff. This smell, and the fact that I caught Dinou looking at me, plunged me into a state of grace. A little boy dressed as a girl rang a bell and everybody looked up. After singing one last song, the people left. Dinou walked out in front of me. She took the hand of a man who must have been her father, and who pulled his cap down over his eyes as soon as he was out the door.

The water in the river was still low, but spring was not far away. Victor, the old man and I were sitting on the bank. The sun was shining and the birds were singing. Our stomachs were full. Mémé had tried out a new recipe for rabbit and I had gorged myself. I was throwing stones in the water to make rings. Victor was dozing with his hat over his eyes. The old man was smoking his pipe.

I watched the rings grow into large concentric circles and I let my mind wander. I wasn't hungry, I wasn't cold, it was a beautiful day, and yet there was a war on, and yet bombs had fallen the other night on Grenoble. Innocent people had been killed. Children had lost their mamas, and mamas had seen their children die. It was too stupid, too cruel, but in spite of this, it was a beautiful day, the water in the river was clear, and I wasn't hungry. It must be easy not to think about other people when you're happy, but I couldn't do it. When I was very little Mickey the Tailor had explained to me that we're not alone, that other people exist, and that happiness is shared. I decided that when I grew up I would be very careful not to get in the habit of thinking only of my own happiness. There were too many things in the world that weren't right, and it would be wrong for me to live my life as if they didn't exist.

The old man was sunk in an abyss of thought, which did not make him cheerful. He gave a little cough to attract Victor's attention. He obviously needed to talk to him. His son's perpetual drowsiness annoyed him. Victor was always lying down with his hat over his eyes. After containing himself for a long time, the old man picked up the hat and shouted in his son's ears, "That's the last time your mother drags me to mass!"

Victor started and sat up. When he was awake, he stretched and yawned. I forced myself not to laugh.

"You say that every week. . . ."

Victor took his hat out of the old man's hands and put it on his head. Victor could not live without his hat. It made him look more important.

Pépé stiffened. He was bursting. It had to come out. "This time I mean it!"

He kicked a pebble furiously and began to walk straight ahead. Victor hesitated, heaved a sigh, and followed him. I did the same. The old man was talking very loud and gesticulating.

"He's a Red, her priest! He's there to say mass, not to talk politics from the pulpit! If he wants to get mixed up in the war, all he has to do is take off his cassock and join the Resistance! They're plenty of priests in town who have nothing to eat who would be very glad to take his place."

The old man was walking so fast that Victor had a

hard time keeping up with him, and I was forced to run. He was puffing on his pipe.

"We all know that Christ was a Jew . . . Must he keep reminding us of it all the time? Besides, what proof is there that he was? The people who say he was weren't there to see him!"

He was shouting. He stopped walking. He was running out of wind. He was very upset. I took his hand. Victor, who had been holding himself back, burst out laughing. This made the old man angrier. I thought he was going to raise his hand against his son. Victor finally stopped, excused himself, and said that it was nerves. The old man looked at Victor skeptically but accepted the explanation. He asked him what he thought, but Victor had stopped thinking a long time ago.

"You have an opinion, don't you?"

Victor refused to take sides. He was against his father's ideas because he didn't believe in taking a stand. He had asked his father to stop belonging to the Legion, not because he was against it, but in case the Germans lost the war, there was no point in having a father who was a collaborator.

"You ought not to think, Papa, it tires you. And besides, someday you're going to get in trouble. People are getting wind of your opinions, you would do well to water your wine a little before the liberation."

The old man started walking again. He was very indignant.

"Water my wine! What have I done wrong? Aren't I a good Frenchman? Didn't I serve in World War I? Didn't I give four pints of wine? . . ."

I burst out laughing. He corrected himself and kept on going.

". . . Four pints of blood for France . . . Me! France for the French, that's my opinion!"

After a long silence, which nobody broke, he repeated in a low voice, "France for the French."

"France for the French." That was his opinion. He would stick to it. He summed up two thousand years of French history in this unassailable little phrase which laid balm to his heart and gave him the certainty of being right. He always brought it out as a last resort, so he could have the last word. It was always followed by a silence which he slowly savored and which he used to recover his calm.

I, too, was French. I felt French. I spoke French. Besides, Mickey the Tailor had told me so. I was Jewish and I was French. So the old man's conclusion didn't shock me. "France for the French": it was right. But I wondered how he could arrive at such an obvious conclusion and go on talking nonsense the rest of the time.

The old man was silent. His step had slowed. His face had become peaceful again. He had fought well. He was pleased. Kinou did his business against a tree and this added to his satisfaction. His conscience was clear and Kinou had "performed." The day had started badly but it was ending well. Dusk was falling. It was a nice evening. We walked back to the house.

• • • •

The old man was listening to Philippe Henriot, the gentleman who had such a nice voice and who always spoke against the Jews. Mémé was knitting. I was doing my homework. Suzanne was looking fondly at Victor,

[52]

who was snoring in an armchair. Kinou was lying in front of the fire with his head on his paws.

Philippe Henriot had finished. The old man had turned off the radio. I listened to the scratching of my pen in my notebook, punctuated by Victor's snores. The old man was thinking. He was always thinking. He was the only person in the house who thought. He got up, walked a few steps, hesitated, and took me by the hand.

We walked upstairs in silence. I wondered what he wanted. I thought he wanted to take me to his room to tell me something. But we passed his room and kept on climbing the stairs. We came to the attic. I had never been there before. The old man stooped over as he walked in, for the ceiling was low. I looked around in wonder. There were wrinkled, yellow apples that smelled good, jars of preserves, big trunks that I longed to open to see what was inside, an old bicycle that was all rusty, a thousand curious objects whose secrets I promised myself I would discover. I had left the old man and I was running from one end of the attic to the other. I had come to a standstill in front of an old broken rubber ball, when my attention was attracted by a familiar sound.

It was the call signal of Radio London. My parents listened to it every evening and I remembered that the speaker often defended the Jews. The old man was holding his ear against the speaker. His face was worried. The speaker announced the advance of the Russian troops and commented that the day of the Allied landing was approaching. My heart beat very loud. I was afraid that the old man would notice my joy, so I sat on his lap with my back to him. I thought about my parents. They must be listening too. They must be hoping like me, and they must be thinking about me just as I was thinking about them. I was so excited that I forgot the treasures in the attic. I turned toward the old man, being very careful not to let him see my feelings. He was very sad and I realized that I must love him very much, for his sadness hurt me.

The speaker kept saying, "The carrots are cooked. The carrots are cooked."

The old man switched off the radio angrily. "For whom?"

I got off his lap. He got up. "Rubbish. You mustn't believe it, my little rabbit."

He put a cover over the radio set to conceal it. He shook his head. He was convinced that it really was rubbish, but I knew it wasn't. We went downstairs, but only after he had promised me that we would come to the attic again and that he would open the trunks and show me what was inside them.

I was kneeling and saying my prayer. I knew it perfectly. When I said "Hail, Mary," I thought of Dinou, whom she resembled so closely. Mémé, who always attended the ceremony, must have thought I was pious. When I was done she kissed me and went out, after putting my pot under the bed. I had placed the watch that my father had given me under the picture of my parents. Its ticktock reassured me. Spring was not far away. I would go swimming in the river. The end of the war was approaching. Soon I would see my parents again. The old people were good to me. And there was Dinou. I was not as unhappy as I had been at first and

I told myself that all I had to do was be patient and everything would work out in the end.

That night the old man slept very badly. He got up several times in the night. The news had upset him.

The next morning on the way to school I met Dinou on the road. I felt rather shy and so did she. It was the first time we had ever been alone. I couldn't think of anything to say, so I asked her how she got the name Dinou, thinking there must be a reason for it. She got all red and said that when she was a little girl her parents had been very worried because she never talked.

They were always saying to her, *"Dis-nous . . . Dis-nous . . . mais dis-nous quelque chose."** And the nickname had stuck. This story made me laugh and I told her that Dinou was a very pretty name. To tell the truth, if her name had been Félicie, I would have thought *that* was a very pretty name too. Everything about her seemed perfect. Even when she made blots in her notebook, I thought they looked very pretty. Just because she wasn't mute anymore didn't mean she was a chatterbox, and we walked on in silence. I watched her out of the corner of my eye. Her gestures always seemed to be in slow motion. I forced myself to walk as slowly as she did so as not to disturb her, and as if I were afraid she would come out of her dream and disappear. Suddenly Dinou took my hand and pulled me away. We had taken a shortcut through the woods and Dinou stopped in front of a shrub. A nest with some titmouse eggs in it was sitting between two branches. Since she didn't talk very much, all she said was, "Titmouse."

* Tell us . . . tell us . . . tell us something—*Translator.*

She looked very happy. She had shared her secret with me. We stood for a long time looking at the nest. We were still holding hands and we forgot about the time. When we remembered, we ran, but class had already started when we got there.

We were red with shame and from running. We were afraid the teacher would scold us, but she didn't. She even smiled, a real smile this time. Not that mean smile I had seen before, but a real one, slightly sad. I remembered hearing the old man say that a long time ago, during the First World War, she had been in love with a boy from the village. He had died at Chemin des Dames and since then she had lived in the past and had stayed an old maid. Maybe that was why she didn't scold us.

We went to our desks and sat down and opened our notebooks. I listened quietly to the adventures of Roland, who blew his horn before he died at the pass of Roncevaux. The teacher told the story with feeling, as if she were telling it for the first time. And yet at her age, the history of France must not be as interesting as it used to be. I decided that she must be very fond of Roland and still enjoy talking about him. I was very interested and so was Dinou.

A spitball hit me on the cheek. I was furious, not just because of the spitball, but also because I liked her story just as much as the adventures of Mickey the Tailor. A boy with a shaved head was taunting me in a low voice: "Paris brat, scaredy cat."

Another boy with a shaved head took it up: "Paris stupe, nincompoop."

I felt braver than I had the first day and I swore I would make him pay for it. I was patient for the rest of the day. To confuse my enemies, when school was over, I left right away with Dinou. We were on the way home when a lump of dirt hit me in the back. I turned around. Three peasant boys were following me. They were the same ones who had taunted me in class. They chanted in rhythm, "Paris brat, scaredy cat, Paris stupe, nincompoop!"

I saw red and piled into them. Two took off, the other stayed. My anger gave me the strength of ten and I beat him up.

I went back to Dinou, who seemed very proud of me, but didn't pay me any compliments. I was disappointed but I remembered that she wasn't talkative. I took her hand. We had gone quite a way down the road when the same song made me turn around. They were on a little hill out of my reach and were chanting angrily, "Paris brat, scaredy cat, Paris stupe, nincompoop!"

I decided to ignore them and after a while they stopped. Since my forehead was bleeding, Dinou washed me at the fountain. I walked her to her parents' farm and went home. I was afraid of getting scolded, but I wasn't sorry for what I had done. In fact, I was rather pleased with myself. My father always used to say that I would never let anybody push me around and he was right. I walked through the garden to the house, determined to face the anger of the old man and Mémé, and sure that I had done the right thing.

Contrary to my expectations, as soon as they saw that I was all right, they came to my defense, in fact they got very angry at the boys who had attacked me. Mémé's hands trembled with rage as she wrapped the bandage around my head.

"The brutes, the nasty brutes."

But she calmed herself and advised me to avoid fights in the future. The old man was walking round and round the kitchen hitting the palm of one hand with the other fist. Kinou was barking. I was in seventh heaven.

"That's fine, my boy. That's fine. You're a man." Mémé was worried by the old man's enthusiasm.

"That's right, encourage him to fight."

The old man was practicing boxing movements in front of the big mirror over the mantel: "One two . . . One two . . . Pow! When I was your age I knocked down a few, too!"

Mémé had finished with my bandage and snapped at his back, "That's right, give him ideas . . . at the age of nine."

But there was no stopping the old man. He was walking round and round the room followed by Kinou, who was barking louder and louder.

"When I made my tour of France as an apprentice plumber-roofer, my boss found me in bed with his wife. I didn't think twice . . . Pow . . . Pow, I let him have it . . . I was a holy terror in those days . . . Huh, Mémé?"

I realized that he had forgotten about me and that it was his youth he was thinking about. Once again I saw what a child he was and I was torn between a strong desire to laugh and a great feeling of pity. I was calmer than he was about what had happened and Mémé, who

[58]

noticed it, shrugged her shoulders. He turned toward her.

"You used to like it, that I was strong; eh?"

Mémé's impatience melted and she smiled at this memory.

The old man looked at himself in the mirror. "I wasn't handsome, but I was strong."

His excitement had died down. He was walking around the room more calmly. Kinou had stopped barking. Silence fell. Mémé broke it.

"There you are, my little rabbit . . . Run and play, and don't get your bandage dirty . . . I haven't got an extra one . . . And you, go and saw me some wood if you want me to cook your corn."

The old man tore himself away from his memories and took me by the hand.

"At your service, Ma'am . . . Your wish is my command . . . Come on, soldier . . . let's chop some wood."

"Can't you let him play?"

"He'll play with me."

And the old man pulled me outside with him.

• • • •

We had worked hard. A big pile of wood was accumulating beside us. The old man wiped his brow. I was soaked with sweat and took off my sweater. All of a sudden his eyes lit up, and I knew something was going to happen. I was getting to know him.

"What if we played a little . . . for a change?"

"What shall we play?"

"Let's see who can piss the farthest."

I was taken by surprise. I was prepared for anything

but this. Panic seized me. This time it was obvious that he was looking for proof to confuse me. It was hard to believe that he could be as treacherous as that, but I decided to stick to my guns and not give in.

"Don't you want to?"

"No!"

He came closer. He was so disappointed. I told myself that my fears were empty, but I didn't change my mind.

"Why?"

"Because."

He walked away a few steps and tried to hurt my pride.

"Because you're afraid of losing!"

"I don't give a damn about losing!"

"Then why won't you?"

My back was to the wall. Tears sprang to my eyes. I turned away so he wouldn't see how upset I was. He started to wheedle. He must really have wanted to play, for he was really disappointed.

"I don't feel like it."

"At your age you always feel like it."

"No."

He became magnanimous. There was hope in his voice.

"I'll give you a handicap of one yard. If you don't win with a handicap of one yard . . ."

I took to my heels and ran away. I ran for a long time without turning around. I stopped beside the river and washed away my tears. I was tired of being humiliated. I wanted to be a child like any other child. I wanted people to leave me alone. I couldn't stand it. I wanted to talk to somebody. A cow walked by and I addressed her.

"I'm fed up with this war . . . do you understand? What does it have to do with me? . . . What about my mother? Do you think I'll see her again? . . . And what about my father? . . ."

The cow said "moo" and I felt ridiculous. But it had done me good to talk to her. When I was calmer I noticed that it had gotten dark. And since I had run for a long time I realized that I was a long way from the house and that I didn't know where I was.

I remembered that Mickey the Tailor had told me that when you're lost you should always get up on a high place so you can get the lay of the land and find your way again.

I took the steepest path I could find and walked into the dark. I was a little nervous and I began to sing to give myself courage.

I walked with my head down. When I looked up to see where I was, I saw the figures of two men. They were armed and the barrels of their guns gleamed in the moonlight. I stood frozen in my tracks. They walked over and asked me what I was doing there. I told them I was lost. After talking it over, they showed me the way to the edge of the village. They made me swear not to tell anyone I had seen them and I knew that they belonged to the Resistance. Before walking home, I watched them disappear into the night. I told myself that there were some men who fought while others thought only of their own little troubles, and this gave me confidence.

Mémé cried like a child and the old man was nervous. When I told Mémé the reason I had run away, she became very angry with her husband and told him that at his age he should have more sense. The old man reminded her of the scene last Sunday, but she told him that had nothing to do with it and that anyway, they ought to respect my privacy, because I was a modest child and they might give me a trauma. I could not ask for more, and I ate with a good appetite. Besides, their concern about me had given me further proof of their love, and I needed it.

The old man didn't know how to earn my forgiveness, and let me smoke his pipe.

"How's the peace pipe, big chief?"

Mémé shook her head indulgently. I began to cough and handed back his pipe. The old man burst out laughing. I laughed too after I had caught my breath.

Suddenly, the old man put his hand to his heart and crumpled. The laughter stuck in my throat and I thought he was going to die. He spoke with difficulty.

"Mémé . . . Mémé . . . my medicine."

I ran to get Mémé, who had gone up to her room. I rushed into the room. Mémé was closing the shutters.

"Mémé . . . Pépé . . . His medicine . . . Quickly . . . Quickly!"

She was not particularly upset and took the time to draw the curtains. I pulled on the hem of her skirt and rushed downstairs. The old man was still moaning. I looked at him anxiously, not knowing what to do. Mémé still hadn't come. I screamed, "Mémé! Mémé! Come quick! Pépé's dying!"

Still taking her time, Mémé went to the buffet and

took out a bottle filled with a colorless liquid, and a glass. I was peering into the old man's face. He nodded his head feebly. Mémé came over to the old man, filled the glass, and held it out to him. He sipped it slowly and it did him good. I didn't take my eyes off him and began to breathe again. Then he took the bottle out of Mémé's hands, refilled the glass, and handed it to me.

"Drink."

I didn't understand but I was ready to do anything to please him. I took the glass and brought it to my lips without hiding my apprehension.

It was some kind of liquor. I choked and spat immediately. The old man sat bolt upright and laughed hugely. Kinou woke up with a start and began barking. I dashed into the kitchen and took a big drink of water out of the faucet. When I got back the old man was still laughing. I was very glad that he wasn't dead and I started to laugh with him. He took me in his arms and covered me with kisses. Mémé put the bottle back in the buffet. She shook her head and smiled.

"My God, what a silly man, playing jokes like that on a child!"

The old man set me down with a last laugh.

"That's not wodkaka, you know . . . That's not Bolshevik bilge water!"

To calm myself I sat down in the big armchair beside the fireplace and looked at the fire.

• • • •

I was getting ready to sleep soundly that night but an air raid woke me. Once again the sky was red. Once again, people were going to die. I took my father's pocket watch and hugged it to me. The old man's pranks

[63]

seemed ridiculous now. I thought of the quiet strength of the two Resistance men who had been so good to me. I told myself that I was learning many things and that when I grew up I would be able to tell the real men from the rest.

. . . .

I had decided to tell Dinou that I was Jewish. I needed to talk about it and I was sure that she would keep it a secret. To my great astonishment, she said she didn't know what it meant and asked me to explain it to her. I was very embarrassed because I didn't know what it meant either. I told her that Jews were just like other people, but then she asked me why I acted as if it were a secret. This conversation confused me and I was sorry I had brought up the subject. She wouldn't let it go. She wanted to know whether it was a disease. I said it wasn't and that seemed to reassure her. She wasn't talkative but she was curious, and her curiosity was aroused. I was ashamed of my ignorance and I was afraid Dinou would make fun of me. I explained that I didn't know what it meant, but I did know that where there was a war they were hunted down and sometimes they were killed. She asked me if Jews were soldiers and I told her they weren't. She asked me if I were unhappy to be a Jew. I assured her that I wasn't and that put her mind at rest. From that moment on she lost interest in the matter. I was shocked by her ignorance and I begged her never to tell a soul. I made her swear. She swore. Then she took me by the hand and led me to the nest.

She asked me if there was such a thing as Jewish birds. This made me laugh. She shrugged her shoulders. She didn't see what was funny. Then she told me about her cows and she said that she knew how to milk them. This interested me very much and she promised to teach me. She invited me to her house. Her papa was there and she had a little brother who was always picking his nose.

"Want to use mine? It's bigger."

Maxime, Dinou's father, was digging in his garden while his youngest son, who was always picking his nose, calmly watched. Maxime frightened me. His cap was pulled down over his eyes and he didn't seem to be interested in anything. Dinou introduced me to him. He gave me a shifty look and made no comment. His son didn't take his eyes off him and kept on picking his nose.

"Want to use mine? It's bigger."

I never heard Maxime say anything else. It was his only subject of conversation. Dinou conducted me to the stable and showed me how she milked the cows. The animals knew her and let her approach them. I was a little afraid of their horns but Dinou's calmness reassured me. She gave me a glass of warm milk, which I drank. Dinou's mother arrived. She hardly looked at me and spoke harshly to her daughter. I thought that her parents were strict with her and I thought of my own. Whenever I met new people, I always compared them to my parents and it was always to their advantage. The only people who stood the comparison were the two armed men I had met in the night. I was sure that my father would have liked them. Dinou's mother told her to go indoors, that there was work to do in the house. Besides her homework, Dinou had to do housework. I thought she was very little for so much work and I felt sorry for her. I told myself that I was a privileged child, and yet my parents were not rich. Dinou said goodbye to me. She was a little sad. I went home. One thing had struck me. Dinou did not look like either her father or her mother. She was beautiful and they were ugly.

· · · ·

Victor's gas buggy stopped in front of the house, as it did every week. It wasn't Victor who drove, but his wife Suzanne. He was slumped in the seat beside her. Worn out from his week, he began his rest cure in the car. Sleep was his favorite pastime, along with checkers. He had taught me to play and I had become his favorite opponent. This was no mean honor for me. The checkers games were important events. Victor didn't like to lose. Every time I took one of his men, the old man held his breath and Mémé hummed to herself to ease the tension. When I took two or three at a time, they looked at each other anxiously, Victor pursed his lips, and Suzanne put her hand on his arm reassuringly. When he took one of my men, the old people smiled at me tenderly. We kept track of the games from one week to the next on a pad. It was the old man who kept score. You should have seen how seriously he took his job, as if he were keeping the books for the Bank of France. Every Sunday night he checked his figures and gave us the score for the week-end, and the grand total. At first Victor was ahead for a long time, but I gradually caught up to him, and you should have seen the look on his face. He would go and lie down without saying a word, in spite of my invitation to him to take revenge. The old man commented on the match, in a whisper. Suzanne blamed Victor's bad form on the fatigue accumulated during the week. And Mémé wanted to put an end to the checkers games, saying that

[66]

they wore her out even more than her work. As for me, even though I beat their son, they didn't hold it against me, they loved me.

"I used to be sharp too." The old man tapped me on the head with his fist. I asked if anybody wanted to take Victor's place, but they all had to do the dishes, weed the lawn, knit. Besides, there's a trick to it, it looks easy, but you wouldn't believe how complicated it is . . . In short, I often finished the game myself, brushing up for my next encounters with Victor.

• • • •

That evening the ceremony took place as usual. I was playing checkers with Victor. I wasn't wearing my bandage any more but only a bandaid on my forehead. The old man was listening to the radio and watching the game. Mémé was knitting. Suzanne lit a cigarette for Victor and gave it to him. She always waited on him hand and foot. In all fairness I should say that Victor had been tubercular and supported his family.

I moved a man. Victor took it but I took four of his. Suzanne made an affectionate gesture toward her husband but he pushed her away.

On the radio a mother in tears was talking about last night's air raid. One of her children was dead. Her house was gone. The old man heaved a deep sigh.

"When is it all going to end . . . and how?"

I took two of Victor's men, then two more, and made a king. On the radio the woman was crying. Victor was pale with rage.

"Papa . . . Can't you put on something else . . . I didn't come here to hear about bombing! I spent two nights in the cellar this week."

I was ashamed for him and I prayed that I'd be lucky enough to beat the daylights out of him.

The old man looked at his son reproachfully. I felt that he must not be very proud of him and that this must cause him pain.

"Aren't you interested in what's happening?"

"Sure, to me."

Victor took one of my men. I trembled for fear he'd see that he could take four of mine. But he was in such a state of nervous irritation that he played even worse than usual. I took three of his men and made another king. Victor was pale. He sucked nervously on his cigarette, which had gone out. Suzanne picked up a box of matches, which she opened wrong side up. The matches fell on the checkerboard. Like the poor sport he was, Victor lost his temper and swept the pieces away with the back of his hand.

"I give up."

Pépé looked at him with a knowing smile. "The way you did in 'forty."

Victor ignored the challenge.

"How do you expect anyone to play under these conditions? Matches on the board, the radio in your ear . . ."

Mémé put away the checkers. Suzanne put away the matches. Victor headed for his room, as he always did at times like this.

"I'm going to hide this game," said Mémé. "They won't find it again."

I was miserable about the whole fiasco. There wasn't a grown-up in the house. I was just as glad that Victor had broken up the game. I listened to the weeping woman talk about her home that had been destroyed

[68]

and her child whom she would never see again. The old man was listening too. I climbed onto his lap and put my arms around his neck.

• • • •

Spring had come. The titmice had hatched. One fine morning Dinou and I found baby birds where the eggs had been. We watched them get bigger and one day we found the nest empty. The titmice had grown up and flown away. This made us sad, but we were happy for them.

Raymonde came to pay us a visit. We weren't expecting her and I was glad to see her. She came by car. An old eleven-horsepower Citroen with a butane cylinder, like Victor's. She was in a hurry and had to leave the next day. In the afternoon she told her father that she wanted to take me to Grenoble where she knew a dressmaker who was selling summer suits on the black market. I was very happy. With a new suit on I would look very handsome at mass on Sunday, and that would please Dinou.

Raymonde drove fast and we were just outside Grenoble. I hadn't been back to the city since I had come to live with Mémé and Pépé. The noise was deafening. I wasn't used to it any more but I liked it. I was a city child. I had been brought up in Paris, in the warm and colorful neighborhood of Strasbourg-Saint-Denis. I thought the people looked sadder than they did in the country, and thinner too. Near the freight station I saw the ruins of houses that had been bombed. This must have been the fire that had made that big red glare I had seen from my window. The woman who cried over the radio, the one whose child had died, must have lived in one of these houses. A German soldier passed and I squeezed Raymonde's hand very hard. Raymonde took me into a café.

I was so surprised that for a second I didn't feel anything. Then I began to laugh and cry and I didn't know where I was. Finally I accepted the situation for what it was and I was overwhelmed with happiness. My father smiled at me, my mother held my hand and wouldn't let go of it. We didn't say anything. We didn't know what to say. I was happy, they were happy. They asked me whether I was being good. I told them I was. It was true. I asked my father for a story about Mickey the Tailor. My father told me a story about Mickey the Tailor's son who went to the country during the war to stay with an old man and an old woman and reformed, after causing his parents a lot of worry.

Two German officers were sipping sodas at the next table. They were very stiff and dignified and were talking in low voices.

I drank my soda. Now that I was with my parents, I didn't think about them any more. They were there and that was enough for me. I amused myself by blowing bubbles in my glass through my straw. It was a game I had played often and my parents usually scolded me, but they didn't say anything.

I asked Raymonde when we were going to the dressmaker to buy the suit but she said that that had been an excuse to take me away from Pépé for the afternoon. I was disappointed and she promised me that next time we would go to the dressmaker's.

I drank my soda. Then I began blowing through my straw in the air. I didn't do it on purpose but when I noticed, it was too late. The straw had landed on the table in front of the two officers. I looked at my parents and they knew by the look on my face that I had done something stupid. It had been a long time.

One of the two officers walked over. He was holding the straw in his hand. Raymonde apologized. The officer handed me the straw, patted me on the cheek, and went back to his seat. It had been close.

All I had to do was see my parents, and I started to misbehave. It must have been my way of proving my affection to them. My parents didn't scold me, but they left soon afterwards, it was too dangerous. They promised to come again.

Raymonde and I drove them to the station. On the platform some civilian inspectors asked to see our papers. Our false identity cards didn't attract their attention, but Raymonde advised my parents not to come again. They agreed, though first they asked me if I understood the reason for this. I told them I understood and that Raymonde was right. I didn't want anything to happen to them while coming to see me. They thanked me, and my father told me that I had become a man, that at least the war had accomplished that much. This pleased me but I let him know that when the war was over I would become a child again and would cause him plenty of worry. My father smiled and hugged me. My mother hugged me too, then put me down and got on the train. I didn't cry. Neither did they. My father had told me that the war would soon be over and I believed him. Before the train started he threw me a five franc piece. I didn't cry but my heart was very heavy when the train disappeared. Raymonde took my hand and we walked back to the car. When we got back to the house it was after dark. The old man asked me why I looked so sad and I explained that it was because the dressmaker had no suits left.

· · · ·

It had gotten so I could almost read his mind. I could look at his face and discover his most secret intentions. I anticipated his rages, his sudden changes of mood, his gaiety, and each new joke he was about to play on me.

We were gathering grass for the rabbits in the fields near the house. It was a rather tricky operation. Rabbits are very delicate animals. Certain grasses that are harmless to other animals are fatal to them. The old man had taught me how to tell these grasses from the others, and I was very careful not to pick any of them.

The old man was soliloquizing about the inconsistency of protecting the lives of these animals when they always wound up in Mémé's casserole. He was very fond of his rabbits and their deaths made him very unhappy. But since there was a victim every day, he tried to get used to it. He said that people were crazy and told me the story of a condemned man with the flu who had been given intensive care so he could die in good health.

I studied his face. I knew he was up to something, but I didn't know what it was. But I decided it wasn't a joke he had in mind but something serious and rather strange. We had finished gathering grass and we were heading back toward the house.

The rabbit hutch was against a wall and about fifty rabbits were crowded in it, big ones, small ones, medium-sized ones, white ones, gray ones, black ones—there was even one that was almost red. The old man knew them

all by name, he knew how old they were, and counted the days until they would have to die. It was because of his affection for them that he had become a vegetarian.

"Here, my little Alfred, eat. . . ."

The old man opened the door of the rabbit hutch and threw in some grass. Some ate without looking at us, others turned their backs on us, but some, especially Alfred, looked at us with real interest. The old man pointed this out to me. He started telling me how cruel it was to treat them this way and blamed Mémé. He couldn't forgive her for the callous way she bled them. He couldn't imagine how anybody could be so cruel. What was the point of hanging around the priest if you didn't respect life? He opened the door of the hutch and picked Alfred up by the ears. Alfred was a little white rabbit who had just been weaned. The old man held him up by the ears and Alfred wiggled his hindquarters. He held him out to me and I took him in my arms. I felt his heart beating madly against my chest. He looked at me with his little pink eyes and I decided that the old man had a point. But still I couldn't forget that rabbit with prunes the way Mémé made it was one of my favorite dishes. I was torn between pity and gluttony. The old man's eyes sparkled and I knew that something was about to happen.

"Let him go," he said.

I obeyed, and after hesitating for a few seconds Alfred took off like—a rabbit, and disappeared into the meadow that bordered the garden. The old man was delighted and clapped his hands, calling encouragement to Alfred. I was very glad myself, and joined in the chorus. I was also reassured, for I decided that the old man had got out of his system the mischief I had seen in his eyes all morning. He threw a final armful of grass into the hutch.

"Here, my Big René, dandelions, nice and tender the way you like them. . . ."

Big René was a nice plump rabbit, sufficiently advanced in age so that his day of reckoning was not far away. The old man sighed deeply and stroked the rabbit's muzzle with a reed.

"Don't get too fat, René. Don't get too fat . . . the boss has her eye on you. . . ."

The old man turned to me as if to enlist my sympathy for Big René's distress. Then a glint came into his eye, a glint that boded no good for me. He had something on his mind, I knew it.

"You know, my child, if you wanted to please me, do you know what you could do?"

He took me by the hand. His expression was pleading and mischievous at the same time. I looked a little scared and I remained on guard. He sensed this and became wheedling. He almost had a sob in his voice: "Do you want to please me?"

How could I say no? It wasn't possible. I found the method unfair. When you want to ask a favor of someone who you know loves you, you don't do it like that. It's not fair, it's an attack on your freedom. You're forced to say yes. I said yes.

The anxiety disappeared from the old man's face, but he hesitated to speak to me as if he were ashamed, as if he knew—which he did—that what he was about to ask me was difficult. I sensed that he was going to be selfish, as usual, and I was right. But he was genuinely upset.

"Stop eating my rabbits, will you?"

At last it was out. He lowered his eyes like a guilty child.

I answered yes, without enthusiasm.

He looked up at me gratefully.

I realized that it was really very important to him. He looked down again, as if he were afraid to meet my eyes.

"Thank you, my child."

He was aware of the enormity of the favor he had asked me. He heaved a deep sigh and walked away. His arms hung very low at his sides. He reminded me of Quasimodo, the bell-ringer of Notre Dame, whom I had seen in a movie called *Notre Dame de Paris*. I caught up with him. We walked side by side in silence. I told myself that I was in a fine mess. And although I had not completely forgotten Alfred, I imagined the smell of Mémé's rabbit with prunes that I loved so much.

"What shall I eat?"

I was really very confused and I wondered what I was going to eat. The old man realized this and tried to reassure me.

"Vegetables, like me. . . ."

Since I wasn't convinced, he added with a bad faith which was only equaled by his sincerity, "Look at the elephants. They eat nothing but grass, but that doesn't keep them from being strong . . . like me!"

As if this argument had given him clean conscience, he lifted me high in the air and laughed his enormous laugh. When he put me back on the ground I asked him whether I could eat chicken, but he answered that chickens were living things like rabbits and that it was out of the question. Reluctantly he agreed to let me eat eggs. And so it was that at a tender age I became a vegetarian.

. . . .

Fragrant smoke was rising from the chimney. It was Mémé's rabbit cooking in the pot.

We were at the table—the old man, Kinou, and I. Mémé came in from the kitchen and set the pan on the table. She lifted the cover with a religious gesture and a wonderful-smelling steam arose. My mouth watered. I swallowed several times. The old man was smiling but watchful. He was afraid of a last-minute lapse.

"Pass me your plate, my little rabbit . . . What do you want today? A thigh?"

I didn't answer and didn't give her my plate, although she was holding out her hand. The old man was observing me. I made up my mind.

"No."

"Would you like the head?"

"No."

"What? Don't you want any? Aren't you hungry?"

"Yes, I'm hungry."

It was true. I was dying of hunger. I could have eaten the thigh, the head, and even the behind of that rabbit. The old man was starting to get on my nerves and I threw him an angry look. But he was so sad. He was so afraid I would change my mind that I smiled at him reassuringly. Mémé was still holding out her hand.

"Come on, give me your plate, my child."

Without waiting for my answer, she picked up my plate. I snatched it out of her hands.

"No."

"What do you mean, no?"

She looked at me, mystified. She was astonished and sad. Maybe she thought that her rabbit wasn't good. She looked at it anxiously. My back was to the wall. I didn't know what to answer. The old man came to my rescue. He pounded on the table with his fist. Mémé jumped and dropped her hand.

"You heard him! He said no! Don't you understand? Don't force him He doesn't want any of your rabbit."

"What do you mean he doesn't want any? A nice rabbit like that, with mustard sauce. . . ."

The thing struck her as so preposterous that she snatched the plate out of my hands in a gesture that allowed no reply.

"Come on, give me your plate."

Now the old man snatched the plate out of her hands and set it before me so violently that it broke. Kinou barked, as he always did when something unusual went on in the house.

"Mustard sauce or not, it's all over! He doesn't want to eat your rabbit anymore! I didn't say a word to him . . . It was he who came and told me . . . He's not a cannibal! Now that he's gotten to know them, he loves them . . . and he doesn't want to eat them anymore. That's what he told me. Isn't that right, child?"

So much bad faith combined with anger disarmed me. I answered, "Yes."

Mémé had sunk back in her chair, but the look she gave me after she turned away from the old man told me that she wasn't fooled. She sighed as she served herself her share of rabbit.

The old man's vegetables hadn't filled me up and in

the night I woke up hungry. Moonlight streamed into the kitchen. I lifted the lid of the pot and took a piece of rabbit, which I devoured. It was a little cold but it tasted wonderful. I went back up to bed, filled with doubts about the capacity of human beings for becoming men.

. . . .

When the old man asked me if I'd like to come with him to Maxime's farm, he didn't have to twist my arm. We were going to get some milk and on the way I swung my pail joyously. The old man didn't like Maxime. He said that Maxime was a very selfish man who had no mind of his own and who traded on the black market. His wife deceived him and it served him right. I decided that maybe that was why Dinou, who was so pretty, did not look like her father and mother, who were so ugly. I was a little sorry that the old man didn't like Maxime, because I liked Dinou very much and was delighted at the thought of seeing her.

She was in the stable milking a cow. The old man congratulated her on her skill and I was amazed to see such a little girl handling such a large animal. She looked at me with her blue eyes and I was off on my merry-go-round.

When Maxime arrived, the old man whispered in his ear as if he were telling him a secret. Maxime's face darkened and he shook his head as if to say there was nothing he could do.

"I have the Ration Board on my back, I tell you . . . You don't understand . . . I couldn't refuse them . . . And when it's not the Ration Board, it's the Resistance . . . Do you think I'm making a profit off the war?"

The old man looked at him with an ironic expression as if he were used to hearing Maxime complain.

"That's what you say . . ."

Maxime fidgeted with his cap. He was obviously embarrassed that he couldn't do the favor the old man was asking him. I wondered what it could be.

The old man seemed to know what he was doing and the ironic smile did not leave his lips. Maxime noticed it and it added to his confusion. His son went by just then, providing him with a diversion.

"Want to use mine? It's bigger."

As usual, Dinou's brother was picking his nose with relish.

Dinou had filled a big pail full of warm and foamy milk. Maxime seized my can and filled it.

"It's hard enough for me to give you milk. . . ."

The argument had no effect on the old man, and he kept looking at Maxime ironically, as if he were sure of himself.

"That's all we need, now that two of us are vegetarians. . . ."

He motioned toward a zipper bag he was holding and began to unzip it with the smile still on his face.

"Come on, be a sport. Just a dozen. . . ."

"Not even half . . . I don't have them."

Maxime's voice was less assured and he had his eye on the zipper bag.

"That's what you say."

The old man pushed the zipper further. Maxime's gaze became more insistent. But he still hadn't given in.

"The Ration Board controls everything, I tell you . . . I don't have any. . . ."

The old man unzipped the zipper all the way and took

out a pair of shoes, which he brandished under Maxime's nose. Maxime seized them up in a flash and laid down his arms.

"Dinou . . . leave Rousette and go and get a dozen eggs . . . and a ham for Victor!"

. . . .

It was a very beautiful day. The sky was blue and the sun was blazing hot. There wasn't a breath of air in the valley. It was harvest time. The men were at work. The reaping machines made a noise that sounded like a huge bumblebee in the heat. The air was so heavy you could cut it with a knife. The grass was dry and yellow and crackled under our feet. The old man, who was afraid of the heat and who was a good walker, had asked me to go hiking with him in the mountain. He had told me we would have a good time up there. We would eat sausage and black bread and drink spring water, and the air would be cool. The old man led the way. Under his cap he was wearing a big checkered handkerchief, which made him look like an Arab. He walked with the steady pace of an experienced hiker. I walked behind him and Kinou brought up the rear. We didn't talk. We all breathed in unison. One remark, one word would have broken the rhythm. The old man had said so. You shouldn't talk when you're hiking. So we walked in silence, without even looking where we were going, our eyes on the ground, leaning forward slightly. We walked for hours. At last we came to a stream. The old man motioned for us to stop. We sat down near the bubbling spring and the old man advised me not to drink until I had stopped sweating. He followed his own advice. We were dying of thirst, but we waited.

He drank first, then let me take his place. The water

was pure and I drank until I couldn't drink anymore. Kinou quenched his thirst downstream, where the spring became a stream. The old man took a sausage and some black bread out of his knapsack. We ate in silence. A pleasant tired feeling had come over us and we felt good. Down below was the valley with the big yellow spots that were the reaping machines.

The old man told me that the first time he had drunk at this spring he was my age. He had brought me on a kind of pilgrimage, and he talked about his life. He talked simply without his usual wordiness, and I realized that his life had been sad, a life without surprises and without love, an ordinary, uneventful life, without direction, a little life. He spoke without bitterness or rancor, as if it were a faraway thing that could not be recaptured; without sadness, either, almost good-naturedly. But the effect was even sadder than when he felt sorry for himself or bragged about himself. It seemed as if nothing that he talked about still existed. Everything was dead. It was far away, the tour of France as an apprentice plumber-roofer. It was far away, the First World War that he loved so much because it was his youth and his only adventure. And Mémé too was far away, very far away . . . the Mémé who had been young and whom he had loved, she was gone, she had become someone else. He put his hand on my shoulder and I pressed myself against him.

"Ah! At least you're here, lad . . . You're the only one I can talk to . . . We won't talk about Mémé . . . We've been bickering for forty years . . . I think it's too late now . . . Even if she stopped eating my rabbits . . . Women are fine, at the beginning . . . Mémé was beautiful once, you know . . . I just got to her in time . . .

Well, she's had her revenge. Now I use her as a crutch. I have a Red daughter who likes Jews . . . A son who's not on the left or the right, or even in the middle . . . Who am I supposed to talk to, my child? . . . Who? . . . Who can I sit down to dinner with? What a farce life is! . . . You'll see! . . ."

I rebelled silently. No, I would not see. For me it would be different. I had wonderful parents who loved me. I'd be good and I'd work in school. I'd make money and I'd marry Dinou. I'd have friends and I'd be happy. My rebellion didn't last long and a rush of pity overwhelmed me.

"I'm here, Pépé. . . ."

He turned to me and smiled. He was on the brink of tears. He was a little ridiculous with the big checked handkerchief that fell over his ears and made him look like an Arab.

"Yes, you're here . . . you're here, my boy . . . But the war won't last forever."

I certainly hoped it wouldn't last forever. . . .

I realized that day that he loved me more than he should and I felt more tender toward him than ever. Kinou walked over to the old man and licked his hand. He knew when his master was sad. When the war was over and I went away, the old man would be all alone with Kinou again. This is what he was thinking as he petted his old friend, I was sure of it. And Kinou was old, very old.

We took our time going back down to the valley. I went to bed very early that night. I was drunk on the mountain air.

• • • •

The end of school was not far away. We were singing

"Marshal, we are ready," without too much conviction, as we did every morning before class. The teacher made us sit down and called on Auguste. Auguste's face did not bear the mark of intelligence. He was very stupid and funny. The teacher called on him often. It amused her. Generally speaking, she always called on the dunces. She took a malicious pleasure in observing their ignorance. And Auguste, dunce among dunces, was the most privileged of all.

"What is today's date, Auguste?"

"The twelfth of May."

"The twelfth of May of what year, Auguste?"

Auguste didn't know and this delighted the class. I suspected Auguste of overplaying the part, for his routine was very professional and he was very proud of his success as a comedian.

"For you it will always be the stone age . . . nineteen forty-four. Thank you, Auguste."

Auguste went back to his seat and it was all the class could do not to break into lusty applause. The teacher looked around the room in search of a new victim. Her smile was terrible. She took her time, slapping her hand with her ruler the way she always did. She couldn't resist calling on Auguste again.

"What is the lesson for today, Auguste?"

Auguste had no idea and this brought on an inane laugh which spread to the whole class.

"Silence!"

The teacher took a map of France and hung it on the blackboard.

"Why am I putting this map on the blackboard, Auguste?"

Auguste was doubled up with laughter. The uproar was at its peak.

"For the geography lesson. Thank you, Auguste."

The teacher tapped on the desk with her ruler to restore silence, then called on Mathieu. Mathieu was like Auguste, only more intelligent, but the difference was very slight. His head was shaved and he was proud of it. With her ruler the teacher traced the contours of the map.

"Mathieu . . . Let's see if shaving your head did anything for your brain."

Mathieu fondled his head affectionately.

"In theory, the air should be good for it . . . All right, Mathieu, what is this area that I am circling?"

Mathieu, surprised himself that he had understood, replied without hesitating, "The map, Mademoiselle."

It wasn't wrong, but he could have done better. The teacher smiled at him with cruel and honeyed condescension.

"Thank you, Mathieu . . . But besides that . . . what is this I am pointing to?"

Mathieu was having a good day. He hesitated as if he smelled a trap, but replied, "The coast, Mademoiselle."

The teacher stretched her neck, which was long, in a gesture of admiration.

"Thank you, Mathieu . . . And why are we going to study the coast of France today, Mathieu?"

Encouraged by his first successes, Mathieu gave an answer which, though not necessarily accurate, brought him huge success.

"Because of the landing, Mademoiselle."

The room exploded with laughter. I didn't laugh.

All this cruelty affected me. And for me the landing meant the end of the war. It meant being with my parents again. I looked at Dinou. She wasn't laughing either. When I asked her why, she answered that she was copying me. I had already noticed that I had a real influence over her. I had often caught her trying to imitate me. It flattered my male pride. Between Dinou and me it was a real love story.

• • • •

I had friends too, by then. I had found boys who accepted me, but I didn't see them very often. I would walk Dinou to the gate of her farm and then go home. My best friend was the old man. He would wait for me on the front step, with Kinou at his side. The time passed slowly for him when I was gone. As soon as he saw me he came to meet me. He always had a joke to play on me. I always had a question to ask him.

For a long time now he had been promising to show me his scar. He was always talking about his scar. It had earned him the Croix de Guerre with Palm and he wasn't about to forget it. Marshal Pétain had presented it to him in person and the undying affection the old man bore him do doubt dated from that day.

We were peeling potatoes in the kitchen. I didn't have to ask him twice. Lifting his shirt, he showed it to me. The scar reigned at the base of the shoulder blade, and was the size of a five franc piece. He let me admire it, then tucked his shirt back into his pants. He was moved and proud at this memory and it was with a gallant air that he went back to his potatoes.

"Yes, my boy . . . A memory of Verdun . . . A bayonet wound. . . ."

The majesty of his bearing contrasted with the humble

nature of the chore he was doing. And the *plop* the potatoes made as they fell into the basin made me want to
laugh. As I had decided to have some fun at his expense,
I forced myself not to laugh and assumed a serious
expression.

"Were you running away?"

The question left him speechless and the potato he
was about to drop into the basin remained in the air.
At last he pulled himself together, swallowed, and per-
mitted himself an indulgent and superior little laugh.

"What do you mean, was I running away?"

I put on my most naïve expression and answered in an
insidiously neutral tone, "Well . . . you were hit in the
back. . . ."

The potato went *plop* as it fell into the basin. The
old man put down his knife. He was horribly upset. I
must have hit him in a sensitive spot, and I was almost
beginning to reproach myself for casting doubt on his
greatest claim to fame. I noticed a kind of panic in his
eyes and I forced myself to erase the slightest trace of
irony from mine.

"Well . . . Yes, I was hit in the back . . . But I wasn't
running away!"

With this last remark, which he pronounced with terrible conviction, he rose and acted out the scene for me.
He was so believable that I could almost see a horde of
soldiers attacking him with their bayonets aimed.

"I was surrounded . . . I was hit in the back . . . but
I wasn't running away!"

He stopped and looked at me pityingly. In spite of all
the love he had for me, I think that at that moment he
really resented me.

"I'd like to have seen you in my place!"

The remark fell like a cleaver and I couldn't think of anything to say. Pressing his advantage, he lifted his shirt again and showed me another scar located above the stomach.

"And what about this one, did I get this one in the back, too?"

He wore his scar like a badge. I didn't turn a hair. I contemplated his scar with detachment and a touch of skepticism.

"Oh! That's your appendicitis."

He shrugged his shoulders but I felt that he was more and more vulnerable. He grumbled as he tucked his shirt back into his pants. My expression was as serious as ever. It was a good thing it was.

"What do you mean, my appendicitis?"

"It is. Papa has one too!"

I pointed an accusing finger at him. I was beginning to provoke him and he got angry.

"Your father may have one too . . . but it's on the other side . . . This side is the liver . . . That, I know! . . . I don't need a kid your age to teach me where the appendix is . . . Sometimes I wonder!"

Suddenly he was afraid he had underestimated my knowledge of anatomy, and to distract me, he went back to his potatoes. His arrogance had disappeared. There was a silence. I expected some crushing argument in keeping with his bad faith, but it didn't come. The old man was hurt. He resorted to his advanced age in order to denounce my insolence.

"Young people these days have no respect for their elders." The *plop* of the potato as it fell into the water in the basin sounded ridiculous. He went on plaintively,

"Anyway . . . I know I got a bayonet wound in the liver. I'm the one who got it, after all . . . It wasn't you."

His face closed like that of a sulking child. He wouldn't talk to me anymore that day, in spite of all my coaxing, and I told myself that if I kept on opposing him openly, he'd stop telling me stories and life would be very dull. I promised myself to be more diplomatic in the future.

As a matter of fact, he needed a lot of coaxing the next time, and when I insisted, he retorted bad-temperedly, "You don't believe what I say."

It wasn't that he didn't want to tell me a story, but he had his pride. Fearing I might lose my principal source of entertainment, I begged him.

"Come on, Pépé. Tell me a story."

But he said that he had already told me everything and wouldn't give in. Several days went by. He was just as nice to me as ever, but there was a strain between us. That element of foolishness that made our relationship so warm was missing. It was like a lovers' quarrel. It was hard on both of us. He fell back on Kinou and I on my homework. Mémé lamented the state of her two babies, and tried unsuccessfully to bring us back together. The old man was stubborn and the situation was in danger of getting worse when I had an idea.

We had finished dinner and the old man had turned on the radio. Philippe Henriot was talking. The old man was drinking in his words. I climbed onto his lap and listened very carefully. He seemed to be aware of this. When Philippe Henriot had finished, I put my arms around his neck and asked him to tell me about the Jews. The old man looked at me with a grateful smile and his ill will disappeared. All of a sudden he was the same as before. He swallowed, which with him was a sign of intense reflection, and said slowly, "Ah, la la, the Jews . . . That is an inexhaustible subject, my boy . . . an excellent subject. . . ."

So I could observe him better, I got off his lap and sat across from him on my little bench. From where I was I contemplated his heavy mass and rejoiced at the idea that I was going to find out what made it tick. To begin at the beginning, I asked him a simple question.

"How do you recognize them?"

Indeed, the question seemed childish to the old man. He answered it carelessly, as if the answer were obvious.

"That's easy. In the first place, they smell."

Sure of himself, he sat back in his chair and a modest smile flitted across his lips. With a trace of surprise, but being careful not to sound skeptical, I asked, "All of them?"

The old man was categorical, but did not use his powers of persuasion. "All of them."

They all smelled. It was obvious.

Why ask questions like these when the truth has been established forever? Even so, I ventured an argument that seemed to have some measure of common sense. "Even those who wash?"

The question didn't throw the old man but he did take a more active part in the conversation, although his smile was as modest as ever.

"That doesn't have anything to do with it . . . You can wash a goat from head to foot, and five minutes later he smells again! . . . It's in the blood . . . And even if you meet one who doesn't smell . . . or if you have a cold that day . . . you still can't go wrong . . . They all have the most incredible noses! Hooked . . . like a fish-hook. . . ."

With his index finger he drew the typical Jewish nose, as it was represented in anti-Semitic tracts I had seen before we left Paris. I put on an angelic look and asked, "Why are they shaped like that?"

The question took him unawares. He wasn't expecting it. But he kept on looking at me indulgently, which gave him time to think and to answer me with a self-assurance which was equaled only by his bad faith and, alas, his sincerity . . .

"Why are they shaped like that? . . . Why, to catch money . . . because they're good at that . . . They run faster to the bank than they do to battle."

He stopped talking for a moment to observe the impression he was making. I was feigning admiration. He was glad to be the center of my attention. He felt that he existed. I was enjoying myself and I was glad he was glad. He went on.

"It's like their flat feet . . . That's so they won't get drafted . . . but it doesn't keep them from running around making deals."

"But do they really have flat feet, or are they pretending?"

"They really have flat feet . . . but not for business. . . ."

My question amused him. It was clear as day, of course: they had flat feet when it came to war and not when it came to business. I smiled at him to show that

I had understood and that I wasn't very smart. He watched me out of the corner of his eye, savoring his triumph and waited for my next question.

"And why do they cut off the boys' peepees when they're little?"

There was indignation in my voice, and pity for their suffering. He minimized the thing: "They don't cut off their peepees, just a little piece."

I pretended not to be reassured. " It must hurt!"

He ran his hand through my hair to console me.

"They have thick skins, they don't feel it . . ."

I put on a sad look. The old man, feeling the ground getting slippery, mustered his forces. Mémé was knitting in her corner. What was she thinking about? Did she even hear our conversation? I wondered. The old man insisted that Mémé never thought about anything. He filled his pipe and lit it.

"Take their Sabbath . . . every Friday night they have Sabbath . . . It lasts until Saturday. . . ."

Like a studious child trying to get an education, I asked, "What is it like?"

He made a scornful and amused face and waved his hand. Kinou seemed to be following the conversation. According to the old man, Mémé never listened and Kinou always listened.

"A kind of holiday of their own, for their sorcerers . . . They don't turn on the electricity . . . They use candles . . . This saves them money, you see! . . . They eat with their hats on . . . Do I eat with my beret on? Do I? . . . And would you believe it, my boy? On Saturday they close their shops . . . For them there's no question of doing business on Saturday . . . But believe me, on Monday they make up for it . . . They make you pay for their Sabbath!"

I didn't answer. The old man was sure he had convinced me that these customs were stupid. My parents were not religious but they had never spoken ill of religion in my presence. I had already attended a Sabbath. I had found it a little strange, but not any stranger than mass. Thinking of mass made me think of Jesus and I asked, "Was Jesus a Jew?"

At this, the old man's splendid assurance wavered. He didn't particularly like hearing about this story. He couldn't forgive anyone for bringing it up, not even the priest. This point of history cast doubt on his most skillful arguments, and he preferred to ignore it.

"So they say."

He said this in a surly voice, with an anger that was suppressed, because he didn't know whom to attack. I had taken the point and I pressed my advantage. I was very careful, however, not to let any of my satisfaction show. I played the simpleton.

"Then God must have been a Jew."

In his worst fits of lucidity the old man had never gone this far. That Christ was Jewish was bad enough, but God the Father, never. This was too much for him. He crossed his legs in a nervous gesture and sank into his chair.

"Oh, no . . . oh, no. . . ."

I didn't give him enough time to pull himself together and prepare an answer. I pursued my offensive.

"Yes, he was . . . Mémé told me that Jesus was the son of God . . . So if Jesus was a Jew, the Father must be one too. . . ."

[93]

"Oh, no . . . oh, no . . . If you listen to everything Mémé tells you, there'll be no end to it!"

For the first time that evening Mémé looked up and asked what we were talking about. I said to myself that the old man was right that Mémé never listened to anything. Since she didn't have a curious mind, she went back to her work. The old man was walking around the room. I observed him from my little bench. Butter wouldn't melt in my mouth. Every time he made a turn the old man threw me a worried look, as if he were afraid of some insidious question that would add to his confusion. But I said nothing and pretended to be thinking. I was laughing inside. My duplicity was total. It frightened me a little and I wondered what Mickey the Tailor would think of it, he who had always told me that you should never lie. I told myself that there was a war on and that in wartime you didn't have to tell the truth. This thought reassured me and I was sure that Mickey the Tailor would agree. Since nothing more had been said, the old man had sat down and his face was calm. I decided to leave him alone. I had had enough fun with him and I didn't really want to hurt him. Still, there was one question I was dying to ask. I didn't ask it to annoy the old man, but because it really bothered me.

"What have the Jews done to you, Pépé?"

After all, it was true. Maybe he had his reasons for not liking them. Perhaps there were Jews who had done him harm. There were Jews who weren't nice; I knew some myself. It wasn't a good reason to hold all the rest responsible, but after all, it was better than no reason at all. In my love for the old man I hoped that he would give me some explanation of this kind. I promised myself in advance that I would listen very attentively and with an open mind and try to understand. But things didn't turn out that way.

"To me? Nothing! That's all I need!"

He was genuinely indignant at the idea that the Jews could have put one over on him. In fact, this idea seemed so incongruous that it made him laugh. I was disappointed, sad, frightened; I wanted so much to understand. I began to laugh with him. I certainly couldn't stay serious in the face of his mirth, but I really felt like crying. Was it because there were people who didn't even know what they had against the Jews that people were dying? It was really too stupid and too cruel. What could be done? I couldn't do anything because I was too little. But what were the others doing? And what would I do when I grew up? That's what I was thinking about while I pretended to laugh.

· · · ·

The next day was Thursday. The old man was taking his afternoon nap. Mémé was visiting a neighbor. I took advantage of their absence to leave the house. I wanted to find the two men whose gun barrels I had seen gleaming in the moonlight. I wanted to see them and maybe talk to them. I wanted to tell them that I was a little Jewish boy and I wanted them to explain a little what this was all about. I was hungry to understand. They would explain. They were men, I was sure of it. "Men who had something in their pants," as my father, who never used coarse language, would say.

I went deep into the countryside. I wasn't afraid of getting lost anymore. I knew the terrain thoroughly. I didn't know exactly what the Resistance was, but I knew

[95]

it existed. Mickey the Tailor had told me so. He had mentioned it only once, and I held it against him. He should have talked about it more often. It's true that at the time I didn't understand very well and I wasn't as grown-up as I am today. I believed that the Resistance was the struggle of intelligence against stupidity, of courage against fear, of truth against falsehood. The Resistance was goodness, I was sure of it, the true goodness which is strength, courage, and truth. Not the other goodness, that of the old man which was composed of sorrow, bitterness, and cowardice. This didn't prevent me from loving him, but that was my problem. For everyone else he was a dangerous person. I knew it, and it hurt me. There was too much pity in my love for it to be a happy love.

I walked for a long time through the countryside but I didn't meet the two men I had met that night, whose gun barrels had gleamed in the moonlight.

When I got back to the house the old man and Mémé were really worried. But they were so glad to see me back that they didn't scold me. They made me promise not to leave the house again without telling them first. I promised. They had been so afraid that they were even kinder to me than usual. The old man secretly gave me permission to eat rabbit. I didn't have to be asked twice and I did honor to the dish. Mémé was in seventh heaven. She was very proud of her cooking ability. It must have been the only thing she was proud of, and for some time she had been very unhappy preparing her rabbits only for herself. I suspected the old man of becoming a vegetarian largely so he wouldn't have to admit what a good cook Mémé was.

After dinner he took me up to the attic. I made him open all the trunks. He did it cheerfully. I ate one of the yellow apples that smelled so good. It turned out that there wasn't much of interest in the trunks: cloth, old clothes, big books. I was a little disappointed, and when he had finished turning everything inside out, I lost interest. The old man was sorry I was disappointed and looked in vain for some old object that might attract my attention. As usual when he didn't know where to turn, he blamed Mémé who, according to him, should have thrown all this stuff in the river. It just collected dust and served no purpose. I was laughing at his anger and his bad faith when my eye fell on an old book with a leather cover. He leafed through it without enthusiasm and handed it to me, convinced that it was of no interest.

It was an old photograph album. I fell on it, to the astonishment of the old man, and to his satisfaction too. I adored photographs. When I was good my father used to show me the family album. I took as much pleasure in it as I did in his stories about Mickey the Tailor. The picture I liked best was their wedding picture. They were very handsome. They were looking straight into the camera. They were noble and straightforward, a little sad like all intelligent people, and so happy . . . I was sorry I hadn't known them then. But I knew that it was impossible . . .

I had imagined the old man in every situation, but it had never occurred to me that he could ever have been six months old.

The photograph was all yellow and he was naked. He had a big stomach and a little gold chain fell over his navel. At the end of the chain was a medal with the Holy Virgin, the one who looked so much like Dinou. He was already old. To me, he looked already old. But I must have been mistaken. You can't be old at that age.

I heard the old man breathing over my shoulder. He was very glad that I was interested in the pictures, but he was remembering too. I didn't say a word as I turned the pages. From the heaviness of his breathing I realized the effect this was having on him. When I got to the wedding picture, the old man heaved a sigh which said a lot. It was true that Mémé had been beautiful when she was young. As for the old man, it must be said that he had never been handsome. And then there were pictures from the war, pictures of peacetime, pictures of friends, pictures of children. As I turned the pages the features of the old man and Mémé became drawn and they became old. Their children, Raymonde and Victor, grew up. She became a woman, he became a man. Time had passed over them, life too, a little life, the old man's, an ordinary life, without much in it.

I closed the album. We didn't say anything. I didn't dare break the silence. I heard the old man's breathing over my shoulder. It became more and more irregular. He put his hand on my shoulder. I took it and squeezed it. He was the first to take his hand away.

He took off the cover and turned on the radio. I sat in his lap. The reception was bad . . . The announcer kept repeating the same sentence in his monotonous voice.

"London here . . . The French are talking to the French . . . Today . . . this . . . the day of the French nation's struggle for liberation. . . ."

The photographs of his life hadn't made him very cheerful and listening to Radio London wasn't likely to improve matters.

I played my part and entered into his game.

"What kind of propaganda are they going to give us tonight, Pépé?"

The old man shook his head with the air of someone who has no illusions and is ready for anything. Mémé burst into the room. She had come to take my measurements for a sweater she was knitting me. The contents of the trunks were all over the floor. But she didn't mention it, she was so sure that the old man would snap at her. Since she had to get rid of her anger, after she had taken my measurements, she scolded me for listening to the radio. When it came to bad faith, the old man and Mémé were two of a kind.

"Ah! No time to do your English tonight . . . And tomorrow morning you won't want to get out of bed!"

I realized that she must care about her trunks, for I had never seen her as mad as she was that night. I argued that the next day was gym and that it wouldn't matter if I were a little late, but she was not convinced.

"Gym or no gym . . . Off you go to bed . . . Kiss Pépé good night."

I kissed the old man but I asked him in a whisper to make her leave me alone. I wanted to listen to the radio and find out where things stood with the landing. The old man agreed.

"Let him listen for a while."

Mémé threw up her hands but she was afraid to insist.

"Oh, you . . . you're going to make that boy crazy . . . One day the English . . . next day the Germans . . ."

The old man threw her a withering look and hugged me. Mémé went off, shrugging her shoulders.

Because of Mémé's interruption we had missed the news bulletins. It was time for the commentator.

"The carrots are cooked . . . The carrots are cooked. . . ."

The old man set me down and switched off the radio, furious. Obviously he didn't have much use for this expression.

"Again."

I told myself that if this put him in such a bad humor, there must be some reason to believe that the landing wasn't far away.

We walked downstairs from the attic in silence and each of us went to his own room. Since I couldn't fall asleep, I started thinking about our oratorical duel on the subject of Jews, and I began to laugh, a real laugh. I had controlled myself during the debate, but now I let myself go. I laughed into my pillow so the old man, who slept lightly, wouldn't hear me.

When I had stopped laughing I got up and looked at myself in the mirror. I verified the fact that my nose was not large. Then I sat down and checked my feet to make sure that my arches were normal. Fully reassured, I swallowed my laughter and headed for the old man's room. On the way I put a distressed look on my face. The old man's snores carried well beyond the door of his room, but they stopped as soon as I banged on his door. I walked in and Mémé turned on the light.

The old man's nightcap fell over his ears. Kinou was asleep between him and Mémé. Mémé, who never slept, looked at me piercingly.

"You're not asleep?"

Without answering, I threw myself into the arms of the old man, who was still half asleep.

"I'm afraid!"

Mémé, whose mind was clear, asked, "What of, my little rabbit?"

"I'm afraid I'm one!"

Having said this, I began to cry very convincingly. The old man ran his hand through my hair and asked anxiously, "One what?"

Between two completely hypocritical sobs, I stammered, "A Jew."

My answer woke the old man up and his eyes widened. Mémé exploded, "No, lad, you're not a Jew . . . No . . . Don't listen to Pépé!"

The old man sat straight up in bed. He gave Mémé a merciless look. Never, absolutely never, had he told me that I was Jewish. That's all he needed, to have a Jew under his roof.

"I never told him he was one."

As for me, I huddled against him and pretended to be terrified. "I'm afraid!"

I swallowed my sobs. Mémé had gotten up to cope with me more easily.

"Come on, back to bed, my child . . . Don't be afraid. . . ."

She tried to tear me out of the old man's arms but I held on tight.

"No! . . . I want to sleep with you!"

She pulled one way, I pulled the other.

"No, no . . . You won't sleep well with us . . . Pépé snores."

The old man retorted that he never snored and despite fifty years of experience and no few nights of insomnia,

Mémé didn't take up the challenge. As for me, I didn't join the argument.

"I don't care."

As if he were grateful to me for not criticizing his snoring, which he knew was not a figment of the imagination, the old man came to my defense.

"Enough! Let him sleep here, since he's afraid . . ."

Mémé, who felt that Kinou's presence was sufficient, lost her temper and snapped at the old man, "And whose fault is that?"

Mémé's anger took him by surprise and as always when he needed time to think, he repeated what she had said.

"What do you mean, whose fault is it?"

Mémé, who didn't have much imagination and was easily flustered, could only repeat with less assurance, "Just what I say. Whose fault is it?"

The old man slapped his chest. Now that for once he had a clean conscience, he was going to take advantage of it.

"Mine, perhaps?"

But as if his good conscience weren't enough for him, he tried to put everything off onto her. I thought I was going to choke, it was so hard to keep from laughing. But since no argument occurred to him, he resorted to a vague threat.

"Do you want me to tell you whose fault it is?

He pointed his finger at her and Mémé did not insist. But so he would know that she wasn't taken in, she shrugged her shoulders.

"Come then, lad . . . Come to bed . . . You won't be able to get up tomorrow. . . ."

"No! I want to sleep with you!"

[103]

The old man was beginning to lose patience. "Are you going to let him sleep with us or not?"

Mémé was calmer. "But he won't sleep well. . . ."

The old man put me down in the middle of the bed next to Kinou with a violent movement which was not for my benefit. Mémé got the point and backed down.

"Oh, you!"

The old man was sleepy and didn't try to have the last word. He became good-natured too.

"What do you want, there's a war on . . . This is nothing . . . I've been through worse than this. . . ."

I said to myself that he couldn't open his mouth without talking about war. He must love it. Mémé squeezed herself into the remaining space.

"Tell him whatever you like in the daytime, but not at night . . . Children dream. . . ."

The old man was getting sleepier and sleepier and didn't take it up. Before he fell asleep he muttered to himself "There's a war on. . . ."

It was true that there wasn't much room in the bed. Then he began to snore. Mémé woke him up and asked him to move over. He didn't budge and said to me in a thick voice, "There, there, lad . . . you have nothing to worry about . . . If you were a Jew you wouldn't be in my bed."

I had had enough for one night. After they had fallen asleep I went back to my room. I laughed to myself in my bed. I promised myself to keep up this game for a long time, for it amused me very much.

• • • •

The next morning I jumped out of bed and went to the old man's room. I hugged him and petted Kinou.

He asked me how I had slept and if I felt better. I didn't answer and put on a worried smile. Then I walked over to the mirror and looked at myself.

I could see the old man's figure in the wardrobe glass, and after making sure that he was looking at me, I put my hand up and began warily feeling my nose. The old man was looking at me attentively. Finally he realized that my worry had not disappeared. He reassured me.

"Don't worry, lad . . . Look at your nose, it's perfectly straight . . . It's not hooked. . . ."

I stepped back, and balancing myself against the rail of the bed, I lifted my foot and examined it in the mirror.

The old man leaned forward so he could see better. The tassel of his nightcap fell over one ear. His face was anxious and he was squinting because he didn't have his glasses on. I was standing on one foot, struggling to see the sole of the other.

"See, you don't have flat feet. . . ."

The old man's voice was gentle and reassuring. He groped on his bedside table for his glasses and put them on his nose. I put my foot down and ran my hand through my hair.

"Your hair isn't curly . . . Their hair is as curly as a sheep's. . . ."

His eyes followed every move I made. Now it was my ears I doubted.

"No; your ears aren't big. . . ."

He was patient with me and I told myself that the old man was capable of being protective. I ran my fingers over my lips, which were rather pronounced.

"But look at my mouth . . . it's big. . . ."

[105]

He laughed gently and shook his head. "No, it's not big . . . It's tiny . . . Don't worry, you'll have girl friends with a mouth like that."

In the end I pretended to be reassured and I smiled at him in the mirror. He was reassured too. He got up. His long white nightshirt came down to his feet. Suddenly I turned to him and stared. He was putting on his slippers.

"What's the matter, lad?"

I kept staring at him to prolong the pleasure. He wondered what was going on and looked at me questioningly.

"Your nose. . . ."

"What about my nose?"

"Look."

"What's wrong with it?"

He walked over to the mirror, half-laughing, half-worried, and contemplated his appendage. It was completely hooked and corresponded exactly to the description of the Jewish nose he had given me.

"It's like you said!"

"What did I say?"

I reminded him of his explanation and to convince him, I took his head in my hands and turned it to the side so he could see his profile. His nose appeared in all its splendor. He pulled away and patted my head, laughing. But I kept going, stepping back to get a better look at him.

"Look at your hair . . . it's curly."

He stopped laughing and ran his hand through his hair. I jumped up and down as if I were jumping rope.

"And your ears! . . . Look at your ears! . . . They're big . . . and hairy. . . ."

He stepped closer to the mirror and stroked one ear

meditatively. He was troubled for a second. I seized this opportunity to make my meaning clear.

"You're one! . . . You're one of them! . . ."

He frowned, looked at himself in the mirror, pulled himself together, shrugged, and went back to bed.

"If I were one of them, I'd know it."

I skipped. I slapped my hands. I ran up and down the room. I shouted.

"You're one of them! . . . You're one of them! . . ."

Kinou began to bark. The old man patted him.

"Don't be afraid, Kinou . . . Don't be afraid . . . It's only a joke. . . ."

The old man sank back in his pillows and waited, rather gloomily, for calm to be restored.

Eventually I quieted down and the old man decided to smile. Still, so that there would be no doubt left in my mind, he explained. He talked to me kindly, as if he were lecturing a good child.

"No, because my father was born in Dieppe . . . my mama in Nemours . . . and since my name is Dupont. . . ."

I came over to the bed and reminded him that he had told me himself that Jews often changed their names so they wouldn't be recognized. He tried to hug me, he wanted to be done with this nonsense, but I jumped back and shouted, "Don't touch me, you're a Jew!"

There was such sincerity in my voice that the old man was taken aback. Mémé came in and I threw my arms around her waist and buried my face in her skirt: "He's a Jew, Mémé . . . he's a Jew!"

I pushed the game to the limit and burst into tears. The old man was very upset. Kinou barked and Mémé lost her temper.

"What, not again! What are you telling him now?"

[107]

The old man was so bewildered that he didn't respond to Mémé's abuse. She took advantage of the opportunity and snatched off his nightcap.

"I want you to stop telling him stories! . . . Do you hear me? I want you to stop it! How stupid you are! You're the stupidest man I've ever seen."

She got it out of her system. It must have been a long time since she'd done this, and it gave her some satisfaction. The old man wasn't listening. He probably didn't even hear her. He didn't even know where he was. I ran, crying, to my room. I threw myself on my bed and laughed into my pillow. I heard Mémé's steps on the stairs. I was sure the old man was looking at himself in the mirror.

When I was calm again, I went back to his room. I wasn't mistaken. When he saw me he walked away from the mirror like a guilty child. I decided to put an end to the joke, if only so I could use it again. He turned his back to me and pretended to ignore me. He looked as sad as the gorilla in the zoo. His arms hung down very long at his sides. He looked out the window. I walked over and took his hand. I made him promise to tell me the truth. He certainly wasn't a Jew. He swore that he wasn't and told me that I had hurt him. I kissed his hand and we made up. He put on his trousers.

"I realize, of course, that it's not easy . . . There are Frenchmen just like you and me who have big noses and big ears . . . and even flat feet. . . ."

He put on his shirt and rolled up the sleeves. His face was serene again and he was being honest for a change. He was forced to be. He had a big nose, his ears were prominent and hairy, and his hair was curly. This was undoubtedly the first time he had noticed it and if he wasn't pleased at the discovery, he had to accept it.

"Negroes, at least, all are black . . . No problem. Orientals are easy too . . . Arabs too . . . But Jews. . . ."

He made a helpless gesture, and I said to myself that it must be because it was hard to recognize them that some people saw them everywhere. Mémé burst into the room. She saw from the look on the old man's face that there would be no more trifling with the head of the house. She made the old man's bed in silence. He looked at her mockingly. I asked, "Tell me, Pépé, how do you recognize them?"

"You can't," said Mémé.

"Who asked you?"

The old man was not gentle and Mémé swallowed it. The old man paused, took a deep breath, and said, "I can smell them!"

Mémé, who was almost out the door, got her word in.

"Oh, you, you're always better than anybody else! . . . You invented the wheel!"

With this she disappeared. He watched her leave, proud and condescending. I was petting Kinou. The old man sat down beside me. He was very sure of himself and repeated, "I can smell them a mile off . . . And so can Kinou . . . Can't you, Kinou? Can't you smell them?"

Kinou licked my face. I had to smile, and since I had decided to make up with Pépé, I put an end to the game by saying admiringly, "Can you really?"

He made no repy but he could see how much I admired him from the look on my face.

• • • •

The old man and I were fishing. We weren't talking.

Farther downstream Victor, lulled by the soft murmur of the current, was asleep. He had wedged his fishing rod between two stones. It was a magnificent day and I was happy to be with my old friend. I had stopped teasing him for several days now and our relations had settled into a pleasant routine. We got along so well together that we didn't need to talk. We were both holding our rods solemnly and staring into space. We weren't very expert fishermen, and the gudgeon rarely disturbed our reverie. The old man had explained that the great thing about fishing was that you did two things at the same time. On the one hand you weren't doing anything and on the other you were doing something. By this he meant that while waiting for the fish to bite you mustn't do anything. And the act of doing nothing was indispensable if you wanted to catch fish. In short, he loved fishing and was eager to share its joys with me. I wanted to ask him why he killed the little fishes, he who loved animals so much and who was a vegetarian, but I told myself that this would hurt him, and I didn't want to do that. And since I had nothing to do, I thought about Dinou.

Victor's rod looked like a question mark. He had a bite, there was no doubt about it. I pulled my line out of the water and threw it behind me. I ran toward Victor.

"Victor! Victor!"

Victor was snoring. I pulled on his rod. It must be a nice specimen, because I had to pull hard. The fish leaped out of the water and it was a beauty. It struggled like mad and I called the old man to the rescue.

"Pépé! Pépé!"

The old man ran over, looked sadly at the spectacle of

his son, and came to my aid. This is how the pike, for that's what it was, found its way from the clear water of the river into Victor's sack. He woke up and claimed his catch. He laughed at us and said that all he had to do was sleep and the fish came and bit. So saying, he re-baited his hook, wedged his rod between two rocks again, threw his line into the water, stretched out on the grass, and put his hat over his face. The old man and I went back to our places and my thoughts returned to Dinou.

My attention was attracted by the barking of a dog. I looked up and there was Dinou. She was chasing a dog who was chasing a goose. She was trying to get the dog, whose name was Adolphe, to go back to the house.

"Adolphe! Adolphe!"

But Adolphe wasn't listening. He must have had it in for that goose, either that or he liked it very much. Dinou was red in the face and seemed worried. I realized that it was serious for her that the goose had escaped, and putting down my line, I decided to help her. The noise woke Victor and the old man shouted encouragement. I ran like the wind. The thought of being able to help Dinou gave me the strength of ten. The old man jumped up and down.

"Come on, champ!"

Victor was yawning but he was on his feet, watching the race with interest.

I had passed Dinou, who kept calling Adolphe.

But Adolphe paid no attention and ran as fast as ever. I passed Adolphe and threw myself full length on the goose and caught her. She had an evil disposition and bit me. I was bleeding but I didn't let go. Meanwhile Maxime arrived and relieved me of the cumbersome animal. He gave Adolphe a terrific kick in the stomach and shook his fist at Dinou. Dinou was red with shame and I with pride.

As a reward, Maxime invited me to his farm. We picked up Victor and the old man on the way. The old man complimented me and Victor admitted that I could run fast. But this didn't make him walk any faster, and since Maxime respected him, because he was a man of means who lived in town, it took us quite a while to get to the farm.

Maxime entertained us under a vine arbor in the farmyard, where a big wooden table with benches always stood. Maxime's wife wiped some glasses and set them in front of us. She was sad, Maxime's wife, and now I was sure that Dinou didn't look like her. Dinou didn't look like either Maxime or her mother. I found Dinou more beautiful all the time, and I said to myself that her real father must be a very good-looking man.

Dinou was taking care of me. The goose had bitten me on the arm and she was putting disinfectant on the wound. I liked the touch of her hands. I was bursting with pride. I had not only the satisfaction of a successful exploit, but also the glory of shedding blood. She worked with great delicacy and when she asked if she was hurting me I told her I had been through worse.

The old man and Victor were observing me on the sly and talking to each other in whispers. It was the first time I had ever seen them in cahoots. I was sure they were talking about Dinou and me.

Maxime arrived with an old bottle covered with dust. The wine inside it was so old it was the color of gold. Carefully Maxime poured everyone a glass. I was getting worried about Victor's and the old man's mumbling, for Maxime had noticed it and had given me a dirty look. I felt that Dinou was taking her time fixing the bite and though I didn't want to, I told her it was fine. The old man and Victor were paying their respects to the wine and Maxime was keeping them company.

"Another drop, Monsieur Victor?"

"No thanks, Maxime."

Victor wasn't used to drinking and pushed away his glass. But the old man didn't like to drink alone.

"Come on, it's better for the passages than cough syrup." Victor had been tubercular in his youth and consumed great quantities of cough syrup, which infuriated the old man, who believed in the therapeutic virtues of alcohol. Holding the bottle, Maxime insisted that Victor have another glass, and Victor gave in.

"Well, a little one. That makes three."

While Maxime was filling his glass with religious care, Victor looked at his feet: "Well, how are the shoes?"

"And how was the ham?"

"Well, we ate it."

They needled each other smilingly, but they liked each other. Maxime pretended that he had made a bad bargain.

"They hurt my feet . . . If only I'd known they were size eight . . . My ham would still be hanging in the attic . . . and my eggs too . . . I'm a nine. . . ."

Maxime's youngest son walked across the yard, vigorously picking his nose, as usual. Maxime didn't miss his opportunity.

"Want to use mine? It's bigger."

The boy paid no attention and kept going.

[113]

Dinou straightened my bandage and we looked at each other. Victor noticed it and thought it would be cute to call attention to it. Dinou and I amused him. He was slightly drunk and I had never seen him in such a good mood. He wasn't even sleepy. He and the old man exchanged conniving looks and he said to me lewdly, "If you run after girls as fast as you do after geese, you're going to catch some. . . ."

He was pleased with himself and slapped his thigh. The old man did the same. But Maxime was furious.

"Don't sit there like a goose!"

Dinou started. She was shy and Maxime terrified her. I wanted to protect her, but I couldn't do anything. I was furious at Victor.

"Go and feed the pig!"

Dinou got up and walked across the yard toward the pigsty. I was very unhappy for her. There was a storm brewing and Victor decided to change the subject.

"Well, Maxime, when are you going to kill that calf?"

Maxime was still mad and answered drily, "When pigs have wings!"

But since he respected Victor, who was an educated man, he made up for it: "Why should I feed the Resistance . . . or the Germans? . . . I'd rather have my calves die of old age. . . ."

Victor pointed out that he wasn't in the Resistance or a German, but Maxime didn't want to hear about it. His son, was was walking back across the yard, served as a diversion.

"Want to use mine? It's bigger!"

The boy didn't even look at him. He was the image of his father and Maxime had a soft spot for him. He spoiled him and was hard on Dinou. He must have known that she wasn't his and took it out on her. Braving Maxime's wrath, I got up and announced that I was going to see Dinou. Victor whistled admiringly and winked at the old man, who enlightened Maxime once and for all about my sentiments with regard to his daughter.

"That boy will go far, if the little pigs don't eat him. . . ."

Victor and the old man were having a good time. Maxime was furious but suppressed his anger.

I stayed with Dinou, not saying anything, comforting her with my presence, admiring her grace among the pigs.

As we walked home, they pestered me to find out where things stood between me and Dinou. It was not so much my romance that interested them as the effect it had on Maxime. His anger delighted them. They walked ahead of me, laughing until the tears ran down their faces. They were drunk and they staggered. I didn't think they were funny and I walked with my nose to the ground, telling myself that grown-ups ought to be brought up by children. Victor turned around and asked me, "Well, what do you say, little pig. Do you like her?"

He fell flat on his face on the ground but went right on laughing. The old man went over and helped him to his feet somehow. I didn't lift a finger. They started walking again, putting their arms around each other to keep from falling down. It was a dismal sight. The old man was hiccuping.

"Ah! When I was his age. . . ."

"What did you do?"

"Terrible things!"

They laughed twice as hard. I sat down in the grass and let them leave me behind. I wanted to be alone. They were singing with gusto. I thought of Dinou, who was probably getting a scolding from Maxime right now. I was very angry with the old man. He shouldn't have played along with Victor. He should have protected me. I stared stubbornly at the ground. When I looked up the old man was standing in front of me. He was confused and I thought he was going to apologize. He held out his hand and I took it. It was obvious that I couldn't stay mad at him for very long. Hand in hand, we walked back to the house. He was still drunk but he did his best to walk straight.

. . . .

My troubles weren't over. It was Victor's birthday that day. Mémé had prepared a great spread, and the old man had picked the best wines in the cellar. The party continued. The table had been set up in the garden under the big elm. I wasn't mad anymore and I joined in the general gaiety. I decided to laugh at their jokes about my relations with girls and I was rather flattered at the interest they showed in me. Cleverly they managed to make me say that I was in love with Dinou. At any rate, when they told me I was and I didn't deny it, they concluded that it was true. Victor tried to get me to say that Dinou and I had tickled each other when nobody was looking. The old man was convinced that we had played doctor. It was true that at the age of nine, I had never played this game, and I admitted it. Seeing how ignorant I was, the old man wanted to know whether I was a man or not. I was, but what did that have to do with Dinou? Victor, realizing that my attraction to her was more of a sentimental nature, asked me if I had declared myself yet. I said I hadn't and he advised me to do it without delay. When I admitted that she had kissed me, their joy knew no bounds, but when they found out that it was on the cheek, because I had helped her get a good mark in reading, they asked each other sadly what I could have in my pants. Since this remark came from the old man and had a double meaning for Victor, who knew my origins, Victor was seized with such a fit of laughing that he almost choked. Suzanne and Mémé smiled indulgently but didn't fan the flames. When Victor had recovered he poured himself a glass of wine and gave me a friendly pat on the shoulder.

"You're still young . . . Nothing to worry about. . . ."

He drank his wine in one gulp and started laughing uncontrollably again.

"Little pig."

I had never seen Victor in such a state and I began to be amused. All at once, seized by a fit of affection, he put his arm around Suzanne's waist and buried his face in her neck. She gave a little cry.

"Victor . . . Victor . . . You're mad! What's the matter with you?

She was visibly surprised, but her astonishment quickly gave way to pleasure and her eyes shining, she began to drink.

The old man popped the cork of a bottle.

"Another one the Huns won't get."

The wine flowed freely. The sun was blazing hot. A wild atmosphere reigned in the family. Mémé let herself go. I couldn't get over it and I found it funnier and

[118]

funnier. Another cork popped. The old man didn't like to wait between drinks.

"We mustn't run out of ammunition."

"This is a special occasion, go ahead, Papa."

Victor was holding Suzanne very tight and she had let her head drop onto his shoulder. She was smiling suggestively, in a way I'd never seen her smile before.

The atmosphere was such that I finally asked for a drink too. I held out my glass. I was afraid I would be refused. But my suggestion was very well received. Victor poured.

"Let's have a drink among men."

I was rather proud and I drank my wine in one swallow.

"Luck in love!" said Victor.

"Luck in love," said the old man.

I winked knowingly at Victor, whose wife was sitting on his lap.

"Luck in love."

Victor took the hint and nibbled Suzanne's ear. She made little gurgling noises.

It was the first time I had ever drunk wine. The blood raced madly through my veins and I felt good. I was warm. My ears were red. I kept laughing. The old man was pleased with me.

"Bravo, lad!"

Mémé was vaguely worried, but since she had been drinking too, she smiled blissfully. The old man was standing next to her and I wondered whether they were going to start acting like Suzanne and Victor. Victor poured me another glass.

"All right, now tell us!"

"What?"

"Have you played doctor with Dinou?"

I said that I had already told him that I didn't know what it meant to "play doctor." I didn't drink my wine, and I felt sad again. I wished they would leave Dinou alone. Victor slapped his thigh.

"I don't believe it . . . Confess. . . ."

The old man looked at me. He saw that I was sad and to distract me, he got up on the table and began to sing.

"I love my wife til death do us part,
I love my aunts and cousins and the rest;
I love France with all my heart,
But I love wine the best! Long live wine!"

He kept time by waving a bottle. We banged on the table with our knives and forks. The old man surveyed the scene from his superior position. He took a big swig of wine right out of the bottle and began to sing.

"Wine is good for everything
Wine will never fill you up,
Come on, Fatso,
Fill my cup."

He brandished his bottle and shouted, "Long live wine! Long live wine! Come on, all together."

We all shouted, "Long live wine!" and applauded. We made such a racket that Kinou began to bark. The old man got down from his perch, happy as an actor who hadn't forgotten his lines. We had shouted so much that we sat silent. Suzanne took the opportunity to get her word in: "And to think that there are so many poor people. . . ."

She was completely drunk. She was halfway between

laughter and tears. Laughter triumphed. Suzanne's remark gave Victor an idea for a toast. He raised his glass.

"To the poor!"

I found the joke in bad taste. I thought of my parents
who were poor and who did not get enough to eat in the
city. Mémé jumped up suddenly and dashed toward the
kitchen.

"Heavens, my coffee!"

The old man got up too. He called after her, laughing,
"Coffee boiled, coffee spoiled."

Then he turned back to us. "Don't go away, children.
I'm going to go and get the vodkaka."

He gave Victor a terrific slap on the back.

"Today I recognize you! You are my son!"

And he walked toward the house, staggering. Suzanne
and Victor took the opportunity to kiss each other on
the mouth. I looked at them, astonished, and wondered
anxiously how they managed to breathe. Suzanne kept
sighing and I wondered if she were unhappy or in pain.
I had never seen a man and woman kiss on the mouth,
I was very upset.

At last Victor and Suzanne separated. Victor looked at
me proudly, but Suzanne looked as if she were ashamed.
Anyway, she lowered her eyes.

Victor put his arm around Suzanne's waist and they
got up. They were reeling. Between hiccups Victor told
me, "We're going to play doctor."

I watched them walk away, not understanding. I really
didn't know what it meant to "play doctor." I was mad
at Mickey the Tailor for not having told me. I was left
alone with Kinou. My mind wandered. Suzanne and
Victor had disappeared into the woods.

The old man arrived. In one hand he brandished a

bottle of liquor and with the other he was holding Mémé by the waist. I wondered anxiously whether they were going to start playing doctor too.

"It's not Bolshevik bilge water . . . it's not vodkaka!"

He put the bottle on the table. Then he noticed that Victor and Suzanne were absent.

"Where are they?"

I hesitated, I didn't know how to put it. Then I jumped into the water: "They went to play doctor. . . ."

The old man's enthusiasm vanished. He sat down and asked Mémé to sit next to him. He put his arm around her shoulders and kissed her tenderly on the cheek. Mémé was happy. This didn't happen to her often. I was reassured, they weren't going to start playing doctor. I patted Kinou. The old man was daydreaming. Mémé poured the coffee. The sun was still high in the sky but the heat wasn't as heavy. There was a great calm which did me good. The old man smiled at me.

"If only they would make us a little boy like you. . . ."

It was then that I understood that "playing doctor" meant bringing children into the world. I looked at the old man. His face was very kind. I realized that he was sad and that he felt old, that he wished he had a little child for the end of his life. I wouldn't always be here; the war would soon be over. I climbed onto his lap and kissed him.

• • • •

Since the old man was in a good mood, Mémé asked him if we could take a ride in the car. She adored doing this. She never got out of the house and it was her only amusement. I liked it too. We waited for Victor and Suzanne to come back and since they agreed, we all got into the gas buggy.

Since Victor often fell asleep at the wheel, Suzanne had taken driving lessons and it was she who drove. She was exasperatingly careful, and when he woke up, Victor would criticize her for it. To please him she would accelerate but as soon as he went back to sleep, she would go back to her usual pace. I was sitting between the old man and Mémé. We always followed the same route, which took us about ten miles from the house. Mémé was delighted and didn't take her eyes off the landscape. And yet she knew it quite well. The old man always asked her what pleasure she could take in looking at it, and she would answer that it reminded her of her youth. In the old days, when she had good legs, she used to cover the same ground on foot, for they didn't have cars then. That day the old man was very nice to Mémé and didn't pick on her. She took advantage of his good humor, and described the landscape to us in such detail that finally the old man told her to be quiet, that we were old enough to see for ourselves. Mémé heaved a deep sigh, pressed her nose to the glass, and fell silent. Victor snored. Suzanne drove even more cautiously than usual. Her mind must have been wandering, for she had just finished "playing doctor." In the end she drove so slowly that the car stopped. Victor woke up and told her that there was no point going for a drive if they were going to travel at a crawl. Suzanne tried to smile as if to remind him of how affectionate they had been a little while ago. But when Victor was sleepy he wasn't interested in love. Then he announced that he was thirsty and since we had stopped in front of a café, we all got out.

The party was over and we drank lemonade, lemonade that was much too sweet. Victor had a headache and Suzanne gave him some aspirin. She always caried it in her bag. I was bored. The old man was sad. Only Mémé was happy.

Suddenly Victor's eyes lit up and he smiled. Suzanne thought he was smiling at her and snuggled against his shoulder. Victor pulled away and got up. Suzanne released him with a little sigh. The old man asked him where he was going, but Victor didn't answer and acted mysterious. Mémé said that after all if he felt like going to the little boys' room, that was his business.

By the door to the café, near the bar, there was a display of colored picture postcards with a picture of two lovers looking at each other tenderly inside a heart and a legend promising eternal love. Victor selected one and came back to our table.

Still acting mysterious, he put the postcard on the table. It showed a sailor with his arms around a girl with short hair and bare shoulders. From the sly look that the old man and Victor exchanged I knew something was up.

Victor took a pen out of his pocket and held it out to me. He asked me if I loved Dinou. I admitted that I did. Victor said that I should write to her and put the pen in my hands. I didn't see any harm in this and I didn't have to be coaxed. In fact, I liked the idea of sending Dinou a postcard telling her that I loved her. I was sure that it would make her happy. As I thought of this, I sucked the end of the pen. Victor was worried for his Waterman.

"Don't eat my pen!"

I wondered what to write and I decided it was best to be simple.

"Shall I say, 'I love you'?"

"Of course, since you do. . . ."

I hesitated to write those words. They seemed so serious to me. I was moved. It was true that I loved Dinou. I had never thought about it until this second. I remembered the first time I had seen her and how she had been the only one who was nice to me. And the time she had taken me by the hand to show me the nest. . . .

"All right . . . I'm writing it."

"Good . . . let's see."

This is how I came to write the words "I love you" for the first time. It made me feel funny. My merry-go-round had never gone so fast. Victor was reading over my shoulder.

"Write 'Dinou darling' too . . . Write 'love and kisses'."

I was trying to write well. I made a blot, but it didn't matter. Dinou made them all the time. I liked Dinou's blots very much. Victor was watching me attentively.

"There are two s's in kisses . . . Oh, it doesn't matter . . . It's nicer that way . . . And don't sign your name . . . Put a question mark . . . make her guess. . . ."

I didn't want to make Dinou guess and I had planned to sign my name to the card, but I didn't mind the idea of remaining anonymous as far as Maxime was concerned.

"How do you make a question mark?"

"Like the stem of a cherry."

I tried to draw a question mark in the shape of a cherry stem.

"I'll draw a cherry . . . It looks better."

I drew a cherry with an interrogative stem. I was very pleased. Victor and the old man were pleased too. The old man gave the signal for our departure.

"Maxime will love it!"

I had written Dinou a love letter and they were delighted at the idea of annoying Maxime. We were pleased for different reasons, but after all, I didn't like Maxime either. So everything worked out well and I never imagined that it could end so badly.

I wanted to mail the card myself and since the mailbox was high, the old man lifted me up.

Under the mailbox a notice had recently been posted. It announced that in the suburb of Grenoble ten hostages had just been executed. The glue on the notice was still wet. The men had been executed at dawn. I hoped with all my heart that the two men I had met that night, whose gun barrels had gleamed in the moonlight, were not among them. The old man and I lingered in front of the notice. The men who were dead had not shared his views, but he was not indifferent to their fate. As always when he was experiencing an emotion he didn't understand, the old man's body sagged and his arms hung very low at his sides. As always, when I knew he was sad, I took his hand. Victor, who was coming out of the cafe with Suzanne and Mémé, glanced at the notice.

"Come on, old man . . . It's none of your business. . . ."

The old man went with the others. We all got into the gas buggy and Suzanne took the wheel.

That night before I went to bed I wound the pocket watch my father had given me very tight. I needed the friendly sound of its ticktock. My heart pounded whenever I thought of Dinou, or the card I had sent her. As I was dropping off to sleep, I imagined the look on the postman's face—he would certainly look at it—and also on Maxime's—he must not be in the habit of reading love letters.

. . . .

The next morning Dinou was waiting for me as usual by the side of the road leading to her farm. We walked in silence. I was red with emotion. Dinou asked me what was the matter and I realized that she hadn't received my card yet. This thought reassured me and I took her hand. I let go of it when we got within sight of school. We walked into the classroom and everything went well until recess.

I was playing football with my friends. I was goalie. I had just blocked several unblockable goals and my team was pleased with me. An easy ball was coming toward me. I missed it to the amazement of my teammates, some of whom started insulting me. I hadn't been looking at the ball, but at Maxime, who was walking into the school-yard. Short, stocky, his cap pulled down over his ears, he wasn't walking he was running. He walked into the teacher's office. Recess lasted longer than usual. The other pupils were delighted, but I knew that for me it boded no good. I kept letting balls go by, and the captain of the team decided to relieve me of my duties at the half.

The teacher came out of her office, followed by Maxime. She clapped her hands and made us form a square. She was solemn. But this did not mean that she had stopped smiling her eternal smile, which was more cruel than usual. Maxime was beside her. He was fingering his cap. I looked at Dinou. She was calm and didn't suspect anything.

The teacher took the card out of the pocket of her blouse, brandished it high in the air so that everybody could see it, and asked in a honeyed voice, "Who wrote this pretty postcard?"

Her voice was sing-song and almost sweet. She was

taking real pleasure in the situation. In the general silence that followed she asked the question again.

"Who wrote this pretty postcard?"

Pupils exchanged looks. I looked at Dinou. From the distress she saw on my face she suspected that it was me. Maxime was fingering his cap, ready to pounce. The teacher's voice became even more musical.

"Who made these charming mistakes in spelling? . . . Who's the brave soul who signs himself with a frying pan?"

What demon made me do it? I'll never know, but instead of keeping still I signed my own death warrant.

"It's not a frying pan, it's a cherry."

I was demanding credit for my crime. I was proud of myself and I smiled at Dinou, who looked down. I wished I could go over to her, take her by the hand, and tell everybody that I loved her.

Maxime's mind worked slowly. He was still ready to pounce but he hadn't understood yet. The teacher asked me to repeat what I had said.

I took a deep breath so that my voice would carry far, and announced, proud as a cock, "It's not a frying pan . . . it's a cherry!"

The whole class burst out laughing. Only Dinou didn't laugh. The teacher walked over to me and held the card under my nose.

"So it was you?"

"It was me!"

Slowly, the teacher took the clippers out of her pocket. Maxime pulled his cap down over his eyes and leaped. I took off. I ran through the empty space that my absence had left in one side of the square.

Since that day I know how it feels to be an animal who

is being hunted down and who is going to die. A mob was at my heels in Maxime's wake. I can still hear the wooden shoes of the fourteen-year-olds and the kinder-gartners, the rubbers of the smaller ones, the screams of the girls. I told myself that this was a good opportunity to count my friends. I thought about the ones who had refused to join the mob and that gave me courage. I was running as hard as I could. I was fast. With all the rabbit I had eaten I can say that I ran like a hare. But I was doomed. It was Maxime who caught me. He carried me, kicking and struggling, back to the schoolyard.

I screamed. I cried. I didn't care about my dignity. I wanted my hair! Dinou's father wasn't angry with me anymore. He was merely the executioner's assistant, doing his duty. He no longer felt personally involved. He wasn't avenging his daughter's honor, he was simply helping to carry out the sentence. The big red-headed boy held my legs. Dinou's father held the rest of me. It couldn't have been easy, I struggled so hard. I howled.

"No! . . . No!"

But the teacher, her eyes set, holding the clippers firmly, carried out the sentence to the very end. Shorn, I was shorn, innocent, far from my mother, far from my father, shorn. Once an animal has been branded, they let it go in peace. It was the same for me. Dinou's father released his grip, the red-headed boy let go of my legs. He made a mistake. My foot landed in his face. I felt humiliated, desperate, hideous. They had dared to do this to me . . . To do this to me, all for a little postcard, one with a rather nice message. They called this justice! When I stole toys, when I tore my shirt, I deserved the beatings I got. But to shave my head for a little declaration of love ... My hair ... My head ... I touched it, it was naked, smooth. What did I look like? I cried silently, I wasn't angry anymore, I was alone.

The ceremony was over. They were standing around me in a circle. They weren't laughing anymore. I stopped crying and I looked at them one by one. They weren't proud. Even Maxime lowered his eyes. And for once the teacher had dropped her eternal smile. Two or three met my eyes. I said to myself that these were the ones who had refused to participate. It's good to have friends and it's at times like these that you know who they are. There are never very many left, but the ones there are you can count on. Mickey the Tailor was right again.

Dinou was wearing a beret. It was a little too big for her and I had often told her so. She walked over to me and handed me the beret. Then she went back to her place, very small and very straight, and didn't look at me. Maxime hadn't budged. The silence was heavy and now I was the only one who was at ease. Except for my friends, and Dinou. I walked over to them and shook their hands.

Dinou's father said goodbye to the teacher and went away. He walked slowly, and he slumped. His cap was pulled down over his ears and he looked at the ground.

The teacher clapped her hands and we went into the classroom.

• • • •

I walked Dinou to the corner of the road that led to her farm. Now she knew that I loved her. She told me that she loved me too. I was afraid she would think me less handsome with my hair cut off. But she reassured me. I wasn't as handsome but it didn't matter. And anyway hair grows back in. We loved each other. We didn't know what it meant, but we loved each other. We tried to figure it out, to pool our knowledge, to analyze our feelings together, but it didn't work. I promised her that when the war was over I would ask Mickey the Tailor what it meant to love somebody and that I would write and tell her. She said that when the war was over she would be very sad because I wouldn't be here anymore. I told her I would be too but that I would be back. From this we concluded that maybe loving somebody meant being happy to be with them and sad to be apart.

When the time came to say goodbye, I seriously considered kissing her on the mouth as I had seen Victor and Suzanne do, but I didn't do it. I was afraid of being clumsy and of not being able to breathe.

I didn't go back to the house. I put my school bag in the hollow of a dead tree and began to walk. I walked for a long time. When I stopped I noticed that I was very high in the mountain. Down below was the village. Smoke was coming out of the chimneys of the houses. I could see the church and the school, the old man's house and Dinou's farm. There wasn't a sound, everything was calm. I said to myself that in these houses there were people, and that among these people there were those who loved me and those who didn't love me. Those whom I loved and those whom I didn't love. There were the old man and Mémé, Dinou and the friends who hadn't chased me. And then there was the schoolteacher and Maxime, and the ones who had been a howling mob a little while ago. I realized that people like to persecute the wounded, the shorn, the Jews, those

who are ugly, and those who are poor. I wondered why.
I wondered why there were so many who ran with the
pack, I wondered why there were so few who stood their
ground and didn't raise their hand or who raised it to
defend others, or when they were attacked. I told myself that my choice was made, that I was one of these. If
there weren't many of them, that was just too bad. My
father always used to say, and so did Mickey the Tailor,
that there weren't many people in the world that you
could sit down at table with. The world was cruel and I
was finding it out. At my age, children aren't as old as
I was; all they think about is playing and getting in
trouble. I myself, not so long ago, thought only about
playing and getting in trouble. But the war had come
along and I was growing up.

• • • •

I took off my beret. I ran my hand over my shaved
head, and I began to cry.

"What's the matter, child?"

I looked up. Two men were standing in front of me.
They were the men I had met that night, whose gun
barrels had gleamed in the moonlight.

The one who had spoken handed me a handkerchief.

I dried my eyes. They sat down beside me and asked
me why I was crying. I told them my story and they
consoled me. They told me that the teacher was an old
maid whose heart had been broken a long time ago. Her
fiancé had died in the First World War and she had
turned sour. As for Maxime, he was a sad fellow and
his wife made a fool of him with every man in the village.
I stopped crying. I didn't want to talk about what had
happened that afternoon anymore. I wanted to talk

about something more important. I wanted to tell them that I was Jewish. I couldn't talk about it to anybody and I was ready to burst. They would be able to tell me why little Jewish children had to be good during the war.

I talked to them for a long time. I told them everything. They listened gravely, without interrupting me. I was expecting a clear answer. But they simply told me to be good. They didn't have time to explain. You had to go way back in history to understand. I told myself that it must really be very complicated, since nobody could explain why little Jewish children had to be good during the war.

They asked me not to tell anybody I had met them and they went on their way.

I was very happy that I had seen them. They hadn't been able to explain, but I felt better. They had told me that soon I would see my parents again, for the Allied landing was not far away, and that the war would soon be over. I believed them because they were in the war and they must know what they were talking about.

• • • •

When I got to the house the sun had gone down the other side of the mountain.

The old man was cutting his grass when I threw myself, sobbing, in his arms. He stood there in a daze, not understanding, looking at my naked head and stroking it. He picked me up and held me very close. I put my head on his shoulder. I stayed like this for a while. He waited until I had calmed down and then exploded. They were swine, they were Communists, and they weren't going to get away with it.

When we walked into the kitchen, Mémé was perched

on a stepladder holding a pot of jam which she was about to set on top of the cupboard. When she saw me she dropped the pot in amazement. The pot landed on Kinou, who fled howling.

They deluged me with all their affection, all their kindness, two of the old man's berets, his cap, an old cap of Victor's and a plan for revenge.

Nothing was terrible enough to make up for this affront. Maxime traded on the black market, the teacher made mysterious trips on her bicycle: the Kommandantur would be informed of these things immediately. So they didn't like color postcards and love stories? Well, they would have letters in black and white and they wouldn't contain love stories, and they'd be anonymous . . . There would be no need for a question mark! We would see what we would see!

At this point I saw something I had never seen before: Mémé rebelled. Up to now she had been the wife submissive to her lord and master, obedient to her baby, but now fear of trouble gave her unsuspected energy.

She rushed to the ink pot and hugged it to her, shouting at the old man that he would write that letter over her dead body, that nobody knew how the war would end, that everybody would know who had written the letter, that the Resistance was capable of anything, and that it wouldn't make my hair grow in any faster.

It was true, that was the only problem. When would my hair grow back? I took Mémé's side, and the old man gave up his anonymous letters.

In one of those about-faces in which he excelled, he explained that actually it was for the best. My hair would grow in more beautiful than ever. Besides, summer was coming, it wouldn't be as hot, my head would be cool, my thoughts clearer, it looked very well on me, I wouldn't have to comb my hair anymore, no more hair in my soup, the advantages were endless. . . .

I took this opportunity to announce that I wasn't going back to school. They gave me permission. The old man would give me private lessons and besides, vacation was almost here.

What could make a child happier than not going to school? So I was happy in spite of my shaved head, and even though there was a war on and my parents weren't with me. It was during this period that my love story with the old man reached its peak. Unlike Samson, who derived his strength from his hair, I derived mine from my shaved head. The old man had really been very upset. Since I knew I had him in the palm of my hand, I used my power every way I could.

First, I made him agree that before going back to work, I would have to have a few days of rest. He admitted that after the ordeal I had been through I needed some relaxation.

There followed endless games of bowling, ninepins, puss in the corner, leapfrog, blind man's bluff, and cops and robbers, fishing and hunting games, cards, checkers, and cup and ball, seesawing and tobogganing, Basque tennis and ball, riddles, crosswords, Mickey the Tailor stories (not as good as my father's), climbing, swimming, races . . . games of every kind.

In short, after a few days the old man was exhausted. Mémé was worried about him and advised him to take it easy. He snapped at her, told her he was twenty years old, and kept on going. I managed to get him to climb a tree, set fire to a clump of bushes, steal apricots from Maxime's orchard, write love letters to the schoolteacher, and break the windowpanes in Mémé's bedroom with a slingshot we had made.

Eventually he got tired, and at Mémé's insistence, he finally decided to give me lessons. Since I knew him like the back of my hand, I saw to it that the lessons were amusing. On the pretext of education, I asked him who the enemies of France were. His face lit up slowly as if he were trying to prolong the pleasure. Then he observed a rather long pause which he interrupted with a little private chuckle. Finally, he developed his argument with such conviction that it had to be sincere.

"You can't go wrong, lad . . . France doesn't have many enemies . . . There are four, not counting the Huns . . . at least they put their cards on the table . . . When they want to fight they declare war on us . . . With them you know where you stand. . . ."

The old man didn't like the Germans—he had fought against them in the First World War—but he respected them. The idea that the Germans might win the war didn't appeal to him, but since he loathed the Americans, he was resigned to the inevitable. The truth was that the old man desired the defeat of Germany and that of America with equal passion, which obviously was absurd. This kind of reasoning was rather upsetting, and he did did not pass up the opportunity to harp on his favorite theme, for it made him feel completely at ease.

"Let's see, there are . . . the English . . . the Jews . . . the Free Masons . . . and the Bolsheviks. . . ."

I pretended to be highly interested.

"The Bolsheviks who eat children?"

I seemed so eager to learn that at first he looked at me reassuringly as if to say that I could count on it, that is was really the truth, and that there was no doubt about it, the Bolsheviks really ate children. He finished, as usual, with the exclamation "And how!"

He beamed, as if this idea enchanted him. Mickey the Tailor had explained to me long ago that Bolsheviks were very nice to children but I pretended to be frightened to death. The old man took advantage of this and had fun scaring me.

With Mémé's carving knife between his teeth, and holding his hands on either side of his face threateningly, like claws, his eyes glaring, his mouth hanging open, he would imitate the average Bolshevik, and chase me around the house. We often bumped into Mémé on the stairs and Kinou would set up a dreadful howl.

I slammed the door of my room and pushed the bolt. He begged me, putting on a Russian accent.

"Let me in, little French boy."

"No!"

"I won't eat you."

"No, I swear."

"On my head?"

"On my head."

Slowly, I opened the door. With the knife still in his teeth, the old man advanced like an Indian. Then he would leap on me and pin me to the floor. He would raise his knife very high as if he were about to cut my throat. I would howl. I would cry. I would struggle. I was delighted. He still hadn't lost his Russian accent.

"I'm going to eat you raw!"

Then he would throw away his knife, tickle me, and pretend to eat me.

"Yum, yum, yum. . . ."

I would protest and accuse him of perjury.

"You swore . . . You swore, dirty Bolshevik!"

I would regain the upper hand. I would throw him down and pummel him with my fists. Since I went at it energetically, he lost no time getting up and asking for time out.

. . . .

The old man blamed the English for burning Joan of Arc, for having leftist tendencies, for not drinking wine, and for hiding back in the kitchen during the war. He couldn't forgive them either for being Royalists, for the old man was very fond of the Republic.

He blamed the Free Masons for carving naked priests and nuns on the towers of Notre Dame. As for the Jews, he had taught me the lesson so well that I couldn't very well ask him any more questions, unless I wanted him to think I was an imbecile. Even so, I never missed an opportunity to allude to them.

I had talked the old man into wearing a hat like me, to keep me company while I waited for my hair to grow back. We were sitting by the radio, listening to Philippe Henriot's editorial. Mémé came in carrying the soup tureen. She set it on the table and put on Kinou's bib— he was already sitting at his place.

"Come to the table, you can listen while you eat."

After we sat down the lights went out and the voice of Philippe Henriot stopped. The old man fumed in the dark.

"Oh, the swine . . . After all this time . . . Right in the

middle of the editorial! . . . They do it on purpose. . . ."

Mémé got up to get the candlestick, feeling her way in the dark.

"Why couldn't they have their power failures while we're asleep? . . . They really do everything they can to drive us crazy. . . ."

Mémé came back with the candlestick and put it on the table. The silence was broken only by the sound we made swallowing our soup. Just then I realized that what with the candles and the hats that the old man and I were wearing, we looked like people celebrating the Sabbath. I made a tremendous effort not to laugh but I couldn't resist pointing it out to the old man.

"Pépé, we're eating like the Jews."

The old man froze, his soup spoon in mid-air.

"What?"

Then he put it down and stopped eating. It was the last straw. He wouldn't speak to me for the rest of the evening.

• • • •

One fine day, at Mémé's advice, the old man decided to tutor me in earnest.

Mémé was mixing cake batter. I was sitting at the table with my notebook open. I was determined to put an end to the lesson as soon as possible, and since I didn't have any ideas, I entrusted myself to fate. Fate is kind, and it was the morning of the sixth of June. The old man, who was always saying that you should begin at the beginning, began by dictating the date. He was pacing the room, holding a book of natural history in one hand. The importance of his role lent gravity to his face.

"Tuesday, June fifth, nineteen forty-four."

I stuck out my tongue and concentrated on the task. Mémé stopped beating her batter and corrected him.

"Wednesday, June sixth."

"What do you mean, Wednesday the sixth?"

"Today isn't Tuesday the fifth, it's Wednesday the sixth."

Fate, chance, or anyway the Allied landing proved Mémé to be right. The soft music the radio was emitting was interrupted by a news bulletin stating that this Wednesday, the sixth of June, at dawn, the Allies had landed on the coast of Normandy.

Like men who are seriously wounded and who don't feel the pain, the old man didn't react. He put the book of natural history on the table and went and sat in his armchair. It was only a short bulletin and the soft music started playing again.

I don't remember exactly what went on in my head. Great joys also leave you numb. But I do remember the old man's suffering. He was very pale and his fingers strummed on the arms of his chair. His eyes were blank. His mouth gaped. His double chin was triple and his body seemed heavier than ever. Never had the gorilla in the zoo been so unhappy.

"Kinou. . . ."

His voice was barely audible. He had said "Kinou" the way somebody else might have said "My God," or "Mama." He had spoken so softly that Kinou could not have heard him. The radio was playing soft music. Mémé had finished beating her cake batter. I didn't know what to do. I didn't dare get on the old man's lap. I wanted to go and get Kinou but I didn't know where he was.

Kinou must have heard his name. Either that, or he had come to say goodbye to the old man. He dragged himself to the old man's chair and looked up at him The old man roused himself from his torpor.

"Well, Kinou . . . What's the matter?"

Kinou looked at the old man, but it was an effort for him to hold up his head.

"What's wrong, Kinou? . . . Did you hear something? . . . An air raid, nearby?"

Kinou didn't even have the strength to look at the old man.

"Worse than that?"

Kinou moaned. The old man heaved a sigh that would have split a cathedral in two.

"Look at him, he's human. . . ."

Mustering all his strength, Kinou gave the old man one last look, and died.

• • • •

It was I who dug the grave. The old man was too tired. The sun was beating straight down. The earth was dry. When the hole was big enough, the old man surrounded it with a low wall of stones and cemented it. Then he wrapped Kinou's body in a sheet and laid it in the grave with his head on his paws, facing the house, so that he could continue to look at his master.

With each shovelful of stones he threw on the grave, between his sobs, the old man insulted the Jews, de Gaulle, the English, the Americans, and the Bolsheviks, all of whom he held responsible for Kinou's death. Mémé, who was crying too, tried for once to defend them: it wasn't their fault, he was old, he had to leave us. Besides two pots of flowers, Kinou was given an epitaph,

[142]

which was written on a small piece of wood until we could get a little marble plaque. It read, *"To our most faithful companion."*

. . . .

After Kinou was buried, since I couldn't do anything to assuage the old man's grief, I began to think about myself. Things had happened so fast that I hadn't had time to be happy. I told myself that soon I was going to see my parents and that I would never be good again. Since I couldn't show my joy, I looked forward to the nighttime. Then, at least, I was alone and I could be happy in peace. The ticktock of my father's pocket watch rocked me to sleep.

My hair was growing back. I took advantage of my last days in the country without school. I would call for Dinou after school and walk her to the corner of the road that led to her farm. I was expecting my parents from one day to the next. But the days went by and finally I realized that the landing wasn't the end of the war.

Besides, the old man was recovering his spirits. Victor, who could see which way the wind was blowing, had finally gone over to the side of the Americans and he joked about the photograph of Marshal Pétain which still hung on the wall of the dining room. But the old man claimed that all was not lost and that Pétain would live to ride down the Champs Élysées again on his white horse, in full regalia. Victor snickered.

"He'll ride down the Champs Élysées again when pigs have wings. . . ."

The old man was controlling himself, but the storm was brewing.

"And I tell you that he'll ride down the Champs Élysées . . . He'll ride down the Champs Élysées on his white horse. . . ."

He was magnificent. I loved him. I had contempt for Victor, whose show of loyalty was coming a little late. Victor snickered again.

"If he can still get on it. . . ."

The old man controlled himself. I felt that he didn't want to give Victor the satisfaction of seeing him lose his temper.

"Until proof of the contrary, this is still my home . . . and in my home, I decide who rules France . . . And in my home, he is France. . . ."

Victor was annoyed. He had stopped snickering. He tried to have the last word. He pointed his finger at the portrait.

"If you don't take it down . . . I won't set foot in this house. It's him or me!"

There was a silence. The two men faced each other. Victor dropped his arm. And now it was the old man's turn to point his finger at the portrait. His voice trembled with anger and emotion.

"You may be my son . . . but he is my father."

He stood for a long time pointing at the picture. For a moment I thought he was going to turn into a statue.

The old man surrendered on the day of the landing in Provence. He took down the portrait of Pétain. I watched him do it. I was equally divided between the joy I felt and my pity for his suffering.

His arms hung very low at his sides, as they always did when he was very unhappy. And at the end of his right arm, in his blue-veined hand, hung the portrait of Pétain. His voice had aged.

"History has passed me by . . . What a shambles. . . ."

With his free hand he took mine and we went up to the attic.

He hung the portrait of Pétain next to the window, over the yellow apples that smelled so good. I picked up an apple, took a bite out of it, and handed it to him. He reached for it mechanically and took a bite, without taking his eyes off the portrait. Tears ran down his face.

"What a disgrace. . . ."

Since I didn't know what to say to him, I told him not to cry.

"Don't cry, Pépé."

He handed me back my apple and smiled at me through his tears.

"Thank God, France will bury us all!"

He took my hand and we went downstairs.

The old man's moods changed from one minute to the next, and since he had stopped listening to Radio London and listened only to Radio Paris, he had not lost all hope. He gave exaggerated importance to the smallest German victory and convinced himself that the Americans were going to be driven into the sea. To keep from hurting him, I agreed with him completely. This didn't change the way I felt and I had to do some real mental gymnastics to pretend I wanted the same thing he did, when I wanted just the opposite.

One day when his hopes were very high, we went for a swim in the river. It was a hot July day. This part of the river was shaded by a big willow tree, and the water was delightfully cool. The old man was a good swimmer, and to show off in front of me he ventured way upstream. I had just learned myself and I stayed close to the bank. I liked to dive. I pictured myself meeting a trout under the water and catching it with my hand. But this never happened, and I wondered where the fish could be hiding. But what I was best at was floating on my back. I looked at the sky through the branches of the willow, and I was happy. I didn't believe a word of what the old man was telling me and I was sure that my parents would soon come for me.

It was then that I heard the first muffled sounds of distant battle. I realized that the Americans were marching on Grenoble. I swam quickly back to the bank and called the old man.

"Pépé, Pépé, it's the Americans!"

I jumped up and down and waved my hat in the air. I tried not to let him know from the tone of my voice the great joy I was feeling. The old man swam back to the bank too. To impress me, he had gone as far as he could and he was exhausted. He panted as he shook himself and sprinkled me with water. He listened with his old ears, but he didn't hear anything.

"No, lad, that isn't the Americans, don't be afraid, you're mistaken."

But an explosion more powerful than the others forced him to face reality.

"The swine!"

Quickly we dressed and went back to the house.

The noise of fighting was getting steadily closer. The old man didn't utter a word. During dinner he refused to eat a bite. I was faint with hunger, but I did my best to hide my appetite. Once he talked about Kinou and then fell silent again. Mémé didn't say anything either. He turned on Radio Paris, which was as determinedly optimistic as ever. He turned off the set wearily. He didn't believe it anymore.

We went up to the attic. Radio London announced that the Americans were at the gates of Grenoble. I didn't get on the old man's lap. I was too happy to pretend to be sad. I pretended not to care one way or the other. Anyway, the old man wasn't looking at me. His suffering was terrible. On the wall by the window, over the yellow apples that smelled so good, Marshal Pétain looked at him.

The old man refused to go to bed. Mémé didn't dare oppose him and neither did I. I wasn't sleepy either. The fighting was getting closer. A great reddish glow lit up the dining room. Mémé was afraid and we went down to the cellar. The ground trembled under our feet. Airplanes were flying right over the house. Now you could hear the crackle of light artillery. I wasn't afraid. I was standing on a big barrel looking out the air shaft. Mémé was shaking like a leaf and saying her rosary. The old man was slumped against the wall, not moving.

Suddenly he rushed over and grabbed a bottle, broke off the neck with a crowbar, and began to drink. When the bottle was empty he smashed it against the wall. Mémé screamed with fear. I laughed out the air shaft.

He railed at everyone—the Jews, the English, the Free Masons, the Americans, and the Bolsheviks. He even added Maxime. He was shouting and walking around in circles. The ceiling was too low for him to stand up straight, and he looked like the gorilla in the zoo again.

[147]

He threw his cap on the ground and stamped on it. Then he went out, in spite of Mémé's entreaties. He promised her that he would be right back and that they would see what they would see.

When he appeared in the arched doorway of the cellar, I was so amazed that I didn't react at all. Mémé dropped her rosary and murmured with mingled fear and admiration, "Ferdinand! . . ."

It was the first time I had ever heard her call him Ferdinand. Ordinarily she called him Pépé. The spectacle was pretty comical, but it was the name Ferdinand that started me laughing. I covered it up as well as I could. But I had nothing to worry about. Mémé was looking at Ferdinand and Ferdinand was oblivious to everything.

On his head was a cap dating from the First World War. He was wearing an old sky blue uniform. Around his waist was a cartridge pouch and in his hand was a gun. Mémé's emotion was undoubtedly caused by the fact that in this getup he looked like the picture over the mantelpiece, the one that had been taken at Verdun and in which she thought him so handsome. It was in memory of this time, the time when he loved her and she loved him, the time of their youth, that she called him Ferdinand.

The old man was in no mood to linger over memories, and declared that we didn't have a moment to lose. He asked me to help him, and together we pushed everything that could serve as a barricade against the front door of the cellar. I entered into his game and enjoyed myself hugely.

He pointed his gun out the air shaft and asked me

to stand by to pass him ammunition. His voice thundered the arched ceiling of the cellar.

"The first one in is a dead man!"

He fired a shot. It was lost in the roar of the fighting, which was now quite close. Mémé erased the image of Ferdinand from her mind and attacked the old man, saying he would get us all in trouble with his ridiculous carryings on. As always when the situation required, she demonstrated her authority. She left the cap on his head but snatched the gun out of his hands. He let her do it. She threw the gun in the corner and asked me to give her the bullets I was holding.

The old man's arms hung low at his sides. With a sob full of anger and humiliation he said, "France for the French."

Outside the battle was raging. At dawn Grenoble fell.

. . . .

Next morning when I opened my bedroom window I saw the Americans camped in the big meadow next to the garden. Everything was calm. The birds were singing again. I waved at the soldiers and they waved back. Later, when I walked through the meadow to go to the village, they gave me chewing gum. The old man refused to get out of bed.

The village was very gay. Everybody had a flag. The people were on their front steps and the cafés were packed. In the village square the peasants were milling around wating for the parade. All the children were there and I joined them. I didn't hold a grudge against my tormenters, and we played football. I played goalie again and performed well. Happiness made me invincible. The girls were watching and Dinou applauded every time I blocked a goal. The grown-ups asked us to stop playing because the parade would soon be here.

The boys and I and Dinou got up on top of a hay wagon so we could see better. Dinou sat beside me and we waited for the parade, happy to have front-row seats. In the square there were nothing but women and very old people. One man had just turned a hundred and it was a double holiday for him, since he was celebrating both his hundredth birthday and the liberation. He had a stubborn disposition and had refused to die before. He died that evening.

Guns went off and the church bells rang in full peal. The parade was almost here.

I wondered what this parade could be, and I said to myself that no doubt it was the parade of those who had stood their ground during the long night of the war, the parade of those who had kept their eyes open, those who had not lain down like chickens, those who had something in their pants, as my father, who never used vulgar words, used to say, the parade of men whom Mickey the Tailor loved, the parade of those who mean what they say, the parade of those who were as scrupulous in victory as in defeat, of those who are afraid of words, of lies, of pretty speeches and decorations, of those who may not have diplomas, but who know how to read faces, of those who call a spade a spade, the parade of men who see beyond the ends of their guns, the parade of those who drink to their friends who are dead, of those who love peace and hate war (Mickey the Tailor had told me that men who make war love peace. The others don't fight the war but talk about it all the time in the shade of the sycamore trees, after peace has come), the parade of those who aren't afraid of death because they aren't afraid of life, the parade of those who don't say thank you when you do them a favor, and who forget the favors they do, the parade of those who don't feed off of the poverty of others, of those who don't shoot a man when he's down, who cry openly and don't wipe their eyes with a lace handkerchief, who don't always piss in the middle of the hole, who never apologize but who know when they are wrong, the parade of those you're proud to have for a father or a friend, the parade of those who were like the two men I had met that night, whose gun barrels gleamed in the moonlight. All this, and more.

As far as the eye could see there streamed toward me a shouting mob armed with pitchforks and guns, without cartridge belts, with delapidated revolvers, and sometimes with clubs hewn that very morning from living trees. Among them there were some who were like those I had imagined, but they were not numerous. They were not many, the men of the kind Mickey the Tailor loved. I recognized the two men I had met that night, whose gun barrels I had seen gleaming in the moonlight. They marched at the head of the shouting mob and their faces were impenetrable. On the village square, the hundred-year-old man gave the signal, and the old people and women shouted in unison, waving little flags. My friends did the same and so did Dinou. She was proud of her papa, who, God knows why, was marching in the parade. When I saw that Victor was marching too, I looked for the old man but he, at least, had stayed in bed. I hadn't had the last of my surprises, and my astonishment turned into great sadness.

In the middle of the parade was a woman holding a baby in her arms. Her head was shaved. She was young and beautiful and people were spitting on her. The old people were spitting on her. Maxime was spitting on her. They spat on her and made jokes. When I asked why, someone told me that it was because she had loved a German and had had a baby, the one she was holding in her arms. The two men whose gun barrels had shone in the moonlight tried to calm the crowd, but the crowd didn't listen to them. The woman had great dignity and defied those who were spitting at her. One of the two men wiped her face. Just then her eyes met mine and I smiled at her. I took off my cap as a sign of respect and also to show her that my head was shaved too. I hoped with all my heart that I had done her some good. I was mad at Dinou for following the crowd. She noticed it and asked me why I was sad. I didn't answer but I forgave her. We had lived the same number of years, but she was so much younger than me. She couldn't understand everything I understood, everything I had been forced to understand . . . She wasn't Jewish and nobody had told her she had to be good because there was a war on.

In front of the monument to the dead some people played bugles and others beat drums. There was a minute of silence. The mayor spoke. He was a bald, fat little man. He spoke for a long time. After a while people talked among themselves and didn't listen to him anymore. Then one of the two men with the guns spoke. He said little but people listened. As he spoke I looked at the people's faces. They looked better. Nobody protested when the man with the gun declared that there was no great merit in shaving the head of a defenseless woman, no matter what she had done. He added that in the future punishments would be carried out by the proper authorities, and that this was an order. The woman with the shaved head was standing in the middle of the crowd holding her baby in her arms. The man with the gun motioned to her that she could leave. She made her way through the crowd. She turned around many times before she disappeared. But nobody moved. The man with the gun announced that the ceremony was over. The people who were playing the bugles and beating the drums struck up a waltz and everybody began to dance.

• • • •

I had to tell the old man that we ought to go and visit Kinou's grave, to make him get out of bed.

It was August. The earth of the grave was dry. The old man was chewing gum. He spoke slowly, very slowly, without anger. He had forgotten that I was there. He was beyond everything.

"My poor baby . . . I'm glad you can't see what's happening . . . It would break your heart . . . It's making me sick . . . Frenchmen at each other's throats . . . Pétain has fled . . . They're shaving the women's heads . . . The world has gone mad . . . Ah, what I've been through . . . 'seventy . . . The first World War . . . the Popular Front . . . the débâcle . . . the occupation . . . the 'liberation' . . . what a shambles . . . Ah, if only I can die soon. . . ."

He couldn't go on. Leaning on my shoulder, he sat down on the little wall of dry stones that surrounded the grave. I sat down beside him and stopped sucking on my chewing gum.

"I'm here, Pépé."

He took my hand and smiled sadly at me.

"Yes, lad . . . You're here . . . But not for long, alas . . . The war will soon be over . . . Nothing makes sense to me anymore, you know . . . Yesterday, it was the Huns . . . Today, it's the American Negroes . . . Tomorrow it will be the Orientals . . . We'll be a colony . . . Their de Gaulle will be President of the Republic some day . . . Won't that be something? . . . Some day they'll want to go to the moon . . . The world has gone mad. . . ."

He had forgotten the Jews. I was amazed and reminded him of them, no longer knowing whether I was doing it out of affection or malice.

"The Jews will be back. . . ."

He nodded his head sadly and smiled, as if to thank me.

"The Jews will be back. . . ."

We sat for a long time without talking on the wall of dry stones that surrounded Kinou's grave.

• • • •

Paris had been liberated. It was September. I was beginning to give up hope when one day, as I was watering roses in the garden, my parents arrived. I won't describe my joy or theirs. We cried for a long time. The old man was sad, but since he loved me he tried to be gay.

At the feast that followed under the arbor, the old man told the story of the postcard, how much he had enjoyed having me with him, and how I transformed his life. Next, he predicted the future of France, saying it would fall again in the hands of the Jews and finally, of the Communists. My father agreed with him wholeheartedly and I stuffed my napkin into my mouth to keep from laughing.

The day before we left I went to say goodbye to Dinou. She didn't have a titmouse nest to show me, so she took me to a place where there were mushrooms. It wasn't late enough in the season and there was only one. She picked it and gave it to me. It was her farewell present. I walked her to the corner of the road that led to her farm. We stood there for a long time without saying anything. I felt like an idiot holding the mushroom. I kissed her very fast on the mouth and it didn't keep me from breathing. She got all red and began to run toward the farm. She didn't turn around.

It was raining on the village. A September rain, heavy and warm. We were waiting for the bus under the old man's big green umbrella, which was big enough for all of us, him and Mémé, my parents, and me. Because we didn't want to hurt them, my parents and I did our best to look sad, and for the same reason they did their best to look happy. Nobody was fooled but we were among people who cared. The bus came and we got in. Through the open window I handed the old man the pocket watch my father had given me, the one whose ticktock had done me so much good. As the bus drove away the old man and Mémé were left all alone under the green umbrella, which was too big for them.

Bookale